ಹ The Skull Collector ಜ

i

Fiction Series
The Alex Evercrest Series
The River Front
The Girl on The Grill
Missing
Maggot
Racist
Votive Candles
Windy City
Country Road
Pool of Blood
Sins of the Daughter
Body Parts
The Skull Collector
The Vanishing
The Shadow Fighter
Moonshine
Grief's Trajectory
The Magic Touch
Northern Lights
Alex Evercrest Heroine
Alex Evercrest Collection Two
New Direction
Disruption
A Family Affair
The St. Lebuinnus Church Murder

A Brian O'Neil Novel
Hawaiian Phoenix
Moon Curser
Death Broker

The Problem Solver Series
Solutions
Drug Lords
Border Crosser
The Problem Solver Collection

The Taelo Series
Taelo: The Early Years
Taelo: The Golden Feather
Taelo: Journey of Discovery
Taelo: Dangerous Passage
Taelo: Condor Clan Slingers
Taelo: Circumvention
Taelo: The Journey of Sages
Taelo: Collection
Taelo: Future Leaders Journey

A Taelo Story:
White Swan and Quiet Pheasant
The Child's Name
Floating Cloud
Quiet Rabbit
Busy Bee
Little Otter & Talking Wren
Broken Spear
Burley Bear & Meadow Flower
Taelo Story Collection

Science Fiction

Ron Mueller

iv

෨ The Skull Collector ൠ
By: *Ron Mueller*

Around the World Publishing LLC
Cincinnati, Ohio

Ron Mueller

ISBN 13: 978-1-68223-994-0

Distributed by Ingram
Alex Evercrest Model By: Pi03@ShutterStock
Cover Design by: Ron Mueller

Ron Mueller

The Skull Collector

1 Skull Collector

*L*evi lay on the lawn enjoying the concert and playing visual games with the clouds passing overhead. Once in a while one would trigger a memory. He was slowly thinking through and visualizing the first time.

He remembered his fascination with Heather. He was always standing just down from her locker so he could get a look at her when she was getting ready for the next class. It was during the late summer football practice when the cheerleaders came out for their practice that he finally went over the edge. Heather was thrown in the air and then landed on the shoulders of the guy that had thrown her up. Her hair had flown back, and her perfect features had been exposed. Her smile that he was sure was meant for him had closed the deal.

It was the moment that his mind seemed to clear, and he knew what he wanted. He wanted Heather to be with him forever.

He spent the next few weeks figuring out how that could happen.

He found a place in the forest that was at one end of the farm. He prepared the grave. He made sure it was dug neatly and to the proper depth. He wanted it to be a perfect place.

He then waited patiently. The school session started, and he kept watch as he waited for the right time. Then one day Heather came to her locker alone to put her books away. She had just locket it and was going toward the gym with her gym bag.

He walked up and said hello. She stopped, smiled, and asked what he wanted. He replied that he wanted to take her out on a date. Her smile caused his heart to beat twice as fast.

He knew she was going to turn him down, so he took the next step. He pulled out his hunting knife and pressed it against her side and told her to walk out the door and guided her to where he had his old pickup parked.

She said he was hurting her.

He told her to be quiet and walk. He put his arm over her shoulder, and they walked slowly to the pickup. He told her to get in and he slammed the door shut. She tried to open it, but he had removed the inside handles for both the door and the window. He hurried to his side and got in, started the engine, and drove slowly away and headed toward the farm.

Heather reached for the steering wheel trying to make him go off the road.

He pulled the chloroform-soaked cloth from the plastic bag and clamped it over her mouth.

Heather went out as she tried to pull his hand away.

He drove down the lane toward the house and then took the small gravel road that led to the lake and pulled in next to the grave. He looked to make sure his dad was not fishing. He heard the tractor and knew that his dad was most likely out pulling the John Deer multiple row hoe that cleared five corn rows at a time. He knew that he had all the time in the world, and he should enjoy what he planned to do next.

He pulled on his hip high fishing waders to make sure he didn't get any blood on his clothes. He then lay Heather face down and with his hunting knife he cut her throat. He was amazed at the amount of blood that kept pumping out. Every year his dad butchered at least one large pig, and he always hung the pig up and then cut its throat to bleed it. He had not expected so much blood from such a petite body as Heather's.

Once the pulse bleeding stopped, he reached down and cut off her head and rolled the body into the grave. He threw her gym bag down after her. He kneeled down and skinned her head and threw all the fleshy parts down into the grave. He rolled the skull around so he could get a good view from the front. He threw it into the plastic five-gallon bucket that was half full of diluted lye water. He put on the lid and made sure it was against the back corner by the tailgate.

He walked to the lake to wash the blood that was on his waders until he was sure that it was all off. He then took them off and put on his sneakers.

He then filled in the grave and put a layer of leaves and several limbs over it to camouflage it. He stood back and admired his work. It looked like the rest of the forest floor. He figured that by spring it would be unnoticeable.

He drove back to the small barn and looked around to make sure no one was looking and carried the bucket in and took it up to the loft and put it behind some old hardware that had been untouched for years. He would come back in a few days to see how Heather's skull looked.

He went into the house where his mother asked him how school had been. He replied that it had been a great day and sat down for his afternoon snack that she always had ready.

He realized he had been daydreaming when the concert music he was listening to ended and the crowd gave a thunderous applause.

He sat back up and once again looked at the two women he had scoped out.

He gave up on his first selection when it was clear that she had someone with her.

He kept his focus on his second choice. He followed her out of the park and watched the direction she was walking in.

Lisa was walking home after the free concert in the field and didn't realize the mistake she had made until it was too late. It was a long walk home and it was getting dark when she accepted a ride. The driver of the black pickup seemed friendly and as she got in; he asked her where she needed to go.

She put on the seat belt as he requested and gave him her address. She was about to thank him when he sprayed something at her. It was the last thing she saw as the world slowly went dark.

Levi smiled and opened the window on the passenger's side to let the fresh air in. He had perfected using the spray bottle to deliver the chloroform. It sometimes made him woozy, but he had learned to hold his breath while he was spraying his prize with it.

He reached over and pulled the young woman's hair back so he could get a good look at her profile. He liked what he saw and imagined what her skull would look like once he processed and mounted it.

He headed straight to the processing center where he would sell her body for a cool fifty thousand dollars. He would keep the head. This was a deal he had set up with the Body Parts manager that would have her chopped up and sell her body parts. He was sure the he was only getting about ten percent of what her body was worth but for years he had to do the hard work of burying the bodies. Now he was getting paid a nice sum and he walked away with a clean skull.

He had called and let them know he was at the door. The warehouse door opened, and he drove in.

He followed as they took her to the next room, put her on the table and undressed her and cut off her hair and bagged it. They said that he was in luck and the doctor that did the dissecting was expecting her in the next room.

He would take the scalp, the ears, eyes and tongue and facial skin and they would bring back the head for him. They said the boss would bring out the money.

This was his third delivery. He was now doing about one delivery every other week. He knew that it was risky to be harvesting so many skulls, but he was strategic about it and made sure he picked up his targets in different county jurisdictions and from quite different venues.

He had picked up one guy by mistake but decided to collect him anyway. Most of his skulls were of women but he had accumulated three of young men. He actually thought the three male skulls were appealing because they were noticeably larger than the rest of his trophies.

Delivery to this local facility was very convenient, and the money was more icing on the cake then he had ever dreamt of.

He had made what he had at first thought was accidental contact at a nearby bar with the person running the operation. He learned later that he had actually been targeted to be a victim to become some of the body parts but somehow during the conversation he had connected with the person who ran the operation he had asked if the body parts business needed any bodies. He had been invited to bring in a body.

He had been surprised by the change in the conversation but the person making the invitation promised that it was a legitimate offer, and the money was substantial.

He had taken his next prize in and had gotten a tour of the operation and an offer of fifty thousand per body. The arrangement was not only financially attractive, but it was even more alluring because he did not have to go through the effort of digging a grave and preparing the skull. It saved him time and a tremendous amount of work.

His father had died a couple of years before, and his mother had passed away the previous year. He missed them both. They had been good parents. He had fond memories of the many family outings and vacations that they had taken him on during his early teen years. But their passing made it much easier to pursue his main interest of collecting skulls.

He moved from the family farm to an old mansion that he had renovated with the money he got from his parents. He thought it was remarkable that they had saved three million dollars to pass on to him. He smiled as he thought about the fact that they were not only good parents but amazingly frugal.

He hired a professional farming group to run his farm and he had the farmhouse refurbished and then had a rental agency manage it. This provided him with a steady cash stream that allowed him to invest all of his inheritance with a local investment firm.

He figured he would not have to work for the rest of his life and could focus on his fishing trips to Lake Cumberland, hunting in the fall and going to concerts, plays and sports events as he hunted out his next victim.

He felt that he had been rewarded for being good in his early youth.

Hunting for the next victim was the sport that he liked the best because it was done in different venues and the selection varied significantly. He always kept his eye out for that exceptional looker that had great hair and was gullible enough to accept a ride from him.

He knew that his good looks and a reassuring smile were key in getting them to accept a ride.

He was now at the Cincinnati River front attending a concert in the park. He was hoping to get his next prize that evening.

He had an eye on a young Black woman sitting out on the lawn and a young blond sitting almost to the top back of the inclined lawn. They both had the look that he wanted. He liked the Black woman the best and figured he would make a move on her when the concert ended.

Alex was sitting next to Matt and enjoying the concert that had been sponsored by one of the large Cincinnati companies. She let him know that she felt that someone was watching her.

Matt asked her if she wanted another iced tea and that he would see if he could spot anyone that seemed to be watching her.

She thanked him and said she would love a refill.

Matt got up and walked slowly to where the portable refreshment stand was parked.

Levi took note of the tall rather handsome Black man standing up and walking toward him. He remained seated but made sure not to look at him or the young woman who he had been sitting with. He wondered if he had been made.

Matt walked by and went over to the refreshment stand and purchased two iced teas and two chocolate ice cream cones. He casually scanned the crowd on the way back.

When he sat down, he let Alex know that he had spotted three potential guys that were alone and looking over the crowd.

Alex thanked him, took a sip of the iced tea, and said that the ice cream cone was just what she needed.

Levi decided that the blond sitting by herself would be the one he would try to intercept. He would invite her to a treat and if she accepted would then invite her to one of the local clubs for a drink.

He made sure not to look at the Black lady again.

It was his lucky night. The young woman took him up on his offer of an ice cream cone and afterwards a drink. She said that she had a club in mind.

He knew he had scored when she selected the place to get a drink. He needed to play it low key and to be as invisible as possible at the club.

Alex had a feeling that something was wrong. She walked out scanning the crowd trying to see if anyone seemed distressed. She saw several young people mingling and talking. Everything seemed to be OK.

Levi seemed to sense that he was being looked at and made sure to keep his back to the departing crowd. He focused on getting the young lady to accept him as someone she wanted to have a few drinks with.

Alex asked Matt if he would later be able to identify the three guys that he had observed.

Matt replied that he thought so. One had red hair and lots of freckles. One had blond hair and was rather young looking and the other had dark brown eyes and he thought brown hair, but that person had his sweatshirt hood on, so it was hard to tell hair color.

Alex nodded and took his hand, and they walked back to their apartment.

Levi and the lady that had identified herself as Elsy walked to a local night spot that had a small dance floor where they drank and danced until close to closing time. Levi did not want to be the last to leave the bar, so he offered to drive her home.

She accepted saying that it would save her a walk up to Mount Adams.

Levi was thrilled. Once in the truck he sprayed Elsy with his chloroform spray. She went out like a light.

It was three in the morning. He had been drinking iced tea in a whiskey glass, so he was ready for the drive up to Cleveland. He would get there early in the morning and be home to have a late lunch. He had been disappointed when the Body Parts operation moved to Cleveland, but the drive was a minor inconvenience relative to doing everything himself to collect the skull.

He figured when he got back to Cincinnati, he would do Chinese carryout for a late afternoon meal and then spend the rest of the evening preparing her skull.

He drove a little over the speed limit but made sure there were other cars driving faster.

The timing of the delivery went off as planned.

He parked in the alley on the side of the house opposite the main street. Two new guys came out and took her in.

He had a short wait, but he soon left the operation with the money and his head that he put in the large toolbox in the back of the truck.

He was just getting back to Cincinnati when a cop turned on the red lights and pulled him over.

He briefly entertained making a run for it and if he had been out by his farm he would have because he figured he knew how to out fox any cop on the roads there. But he pulled over and kept his hands on the steering wheel.

One cop shouted for him to get out and stand behind the pickup. The other walked up to the passenger window and looked in. He then went around to the driver's side and examined the inside more closely.

Levi hoped that he would not get inspected too closely.

He presented his driver's license and listened to the officer that said he had been doing sixty-five in fifty-five-mile zone. He was asked if he had any alcohol in the pickup.

Levi was glad that he had not stopped to stock up on beer. He only had an iced tea from the big Mac in the pickup.

The officer looking inside of the pickup said it was clear.

He was asked to close his eyes and touch his nose with both index fingers.

He did that with no problem.

The officer nodded and said OK and wrote out the speeding ticket and advised him that he should stick to the speed limit.

The two cops got back into their unit and waited for him to go on his way.

He was so glad that he had no outstanding tickets. He had only one ticket in his life that he had gotten when he was sixteen.

Levi got back into his pickup and drove away doing fifty-five and being passed by every car on the highway. He figured that the cops were getting in their quota of speeding tickets. He knew that the ticket would cost him somewhere around three-hundred dollars, but he was so relieved that no detailed search had been done that he smiled and thanked the lord for small favors.

He then focused his thoughts on the upcoming processing of the head. This was the part he especially enjoyed. He was pleased that the body processing group always wanted the eyes, the tongue, the ears, and the scalp. That made his cleaning of the skull easy, and he did not have to deal with a bunch of waste to dispose of. The disposal had been reduced to scraping the flesh off the skull, boiling that residue, and then putting it down the sink through the garbage disposal.

The rest of the processing involved bleaching the skull and the mounting it. He enjoyed making the small plaque that had the young lady's picture a brief description of his time with her and the date of her beheading.

When he moved into his current home, he had converted the entire third floor into his display floor. It had a beautiful wood floor that had star patterns positioned strategically around the rooms. He had display pedestals made that were then positioned on each star. He had organized all the skulls in order of the date and had put each skull on its own separate pedestal. He was proud of the way he had arranged the layout and the spot lighting for each pedestal.

He wished he could give tours of his collection. He thought of the collection as a show of high art.

Many of his evening hours were spent walking the third floor and recalling the events leading to him getting each of his trophies.

The first floor had an entry area that he had arranged using the same pedestals as on the third floor but instead of heads he had put fake statues of Greek and Roman nude women.

The morning after the conference at breakfast, Alex shared the fact that she had a nightmare about the feeling of being watched the day before. She shared that she had one of her premonitions about the situation and was going to be extra careful for a few days until she could sort out what was going on.

Matt said he would be sure to keep a watch to make sure none of the three guys were around.

She took her bike down as usual and met Johnnie at the elevator. She asked him to pick a route to work that they usually did not take.

Johnnie asked what was going on.

Alex briefly shared what had happened.

Johnnie nodded and said he would pick a different route.

Once in the office, as they all sat down for their morning coffee and rolls Johnnie asked Alex to go into more detail about the concert in the park.

Alex described the situation and said that she had a dream about it and woke up in the morning with a premonition of trouble.

Trevor shook his head and said he hated it when she got her premonitions because so far, every time, she had one the team was faced with a major gun battle.

Trey said that he agreed but that every time they had all been prepared for the resulting gun battle and they, working together, had weathered every one of them.

He added that in every one of those situations Alex had taken the point and led them to victory. He also highlighted the number of times when she had been attacked while by herself and she had taken out her attacker.

Alex shook her head and said that this premonition was different, and the difference was what was bothering her.

The Chief came out of his office and joined them. He shared that he had just gotten off the phone with their friend, the Chief of Police of Loveland who wanted to see if Alex and Trey would be able to stop by around lunch time. He wanted the two to meet a friend that was dealing with three missing young women each who had gone riding or hiking alone in different parts of the county and had never returned home.

Alex shook her head as she wondered if the lunch meeting would lead to what was bothering her. She said that she and Trey would go to Loveland for lunch.

She looked at Johnnie and asked if he was willing to come along to hear the story because she had a bad feeling about the meeting. She said that she wanted him to look for any missing women who had not returned from the concert in the park.

<u>2 A Nagging Feeling</u>

*A*lex sat in the passenger seat of her car as Trey drove to Loveland. She went through each of the previous cases where she and the team had intervened in situations where young women were about to get abused before being killed. It haunted her that during the time it took to break each of those cases young women had faced the situation by themselves, had been brutalized and then killed. This fact always came up when she engaged in a new case and the desire to solve the case as rapidly as possible became a key consideration. She had that feeling now. She was sure that in some way she was going to be presented with some situation that would have her driving the team to move fast.

She smiled as she realized that Trey had detoured to her favorite store and said that he would go in and buy the bags of candy and that he only wanted to know how many bags to buy. She asked for at least a dozen bags, but she insisted that she pay.

She looked back at Johnnie and let him know that one was for him. She wanted him to scan the missing person reports for Hamilton County and every county that bordered it and gather all the ones about missing women. She asked him to keep an eye out for one that had happened in the last couple of days.

Johnnie nodded and said that he would do it, but he wondered if he could negotiate for a tray of her cookies instead of a bag of candy.

Alex smiled and nodded but stipulated that a tray of cookies would mean he would need to set up breakfast each morning for the two of them for the rest of the week.

Johnnie nodded and replied that was an easy ask.

She enjoyed their close relationship and thought of Johnnie as her second father. Johnnie was a few years older than her father. Older but she knew Johnnie was in great condition and was exceptionally strong. He had demonstrated his physical strength when he had lowered a reel of wire cable from the bed of a maintenance truck. He had backed her up when Trey had been in the hospital recovering from near death after being brutally beaten. He had demonstrated his strength by lowering a roll of wire cabling from the back of a maintenance truck and then his bravery by pulling the wire cable off that reel through the legs of the helicopter and tying it to a fire hydrant. When the copter went to take off to shoot at her it crashed to the ground as it tried to take off.

Trey returned with the bags of candy, and they drove on into Loveland.

They arrived at the police station where they were cordially greeted like a part of the Loveland unit.

Alex looked at Trey and commented that a few bags of candy went a long way in making friends.

Sheriff Williams greeted them, thanked Alex for the bag of chocolate, introduced his Friend Arthur Milster, Sheriff of Missteer and asked whether they were ready for lunch. He said that he preferred to have them listen to Sheriff Milster after lunch.

Alex handed Arthur a bag of chocolate candy and introduced Trey and Johnnie.

She then said that she was not sure that ready was the condition she would find herself in, but she was willing to have lunch first and then return to hear the details afterwards.

Johnnie spoke up and said that it sounded like a good plan. He wanted to enjoy the lunch and watch the Little Miami to see if there would be any logs floating downstream.

Alex smiled at the reference to logs floating downstream because this was a Johnnie euphemism for thinking deeply about a case. She knew that he was probably already figuring out how to get the information she had requested.

A short time later they arrived at the restaurant, and they sat at an outside table that indeed had a great view of the Little Miami. It had not rained for a few days, so the river was running calmly by. She figured no actual logs would be floating by.

Alex made sure that Johnnie had a view of the river. She was sure the only floating logs would be in Johnnie's mind.

Sheriff Williams volunteered to order for all of them, and everyone agreed to let him do it. He put in an order for three of his favorite tacos and made sure the waiter knew that he wanted one for each person. He also ordered one tostada for each person. The final order was for three orders of donut holes with chocolate and caramel sauce drizzled over them. He reassured Alex that donut holes would be more than enough for all of them.

Alex joked with him that he would need to let them sleep in his van after lunch to recover from all the food he had ordered.

He nodded and replied that he wasn't worried about any of them falling asleep when they listened to what Sheriff Milster shared with them.

Johnnie nodded and said that he already had a premonition of the story and he planned to enjoy lunch.

Alex agreed and added that she was especially looking forward to the dessert.

Sheriff Williams made sure that the conversation remained light. He asked each person to share a highlight about themselves. He knew that his friend was feeling down and concerned about the fact that he had come up empty handed in trying to solve the cases of three missing women. His friend had worked for almost three years and had come up empty handed. All three cases were now cold, and they hung heavy on his friend's mind.

He knew how that felt because he had carried a similar weight for more than fifteen years when Annie, a young teenager, had gone missing, and the case went cold.

He also knew how he felt when Alex, against all odds, had solved the case and had rescued Annie and her two kids from the forests of Pennsylvania.   Alex had become a person who he thought about often as he followed the cases, she took on that had stumped other agencies and then marveled when she solved them.

He was an ultimate Alex supporter.

Alex enjoyed the lunch, but she would have liked not to be anticipating some horrific case from Sheriff Milster.

After lunch they all rode back to the Loveland police station, to a conference room and sat around a large meeting table. Sheriff Williams had iced tea and lemonade brought in and when everyone was seated, he asked Sheriff Milster to share the situation he faced.

Alex asked Johnnie to connect his computer to the Cincinnati police computer and see if there would be anything like what Sheriff Milster was about to share.

Sheriff Milster said that he liked how fast Alex was planning to try to help. He added that he hoped she would be successful where he had failed.

Alex nodded and replied that she figured he had only bad news to share and that every case in the past that she had taken on had a sad or horrible beginning and she was only trying to be prepared.

Sheriff Milster then described having three missing persons reports about three young women that seemed to have no connection to each other. Each had occurred several years ago but almost exactly one month apart in his jurisdiction.

Each young lady was reported missing, but each had a very different disappearance scenario, and the three did not know each other. The only similarity was that each had gone out alone and had never returned.

He then described the first situation where the young lady had gone by herself to an outdoor concert and had never returned home. She was last seen by some of her friends talking to a young man that was described as dark haired and rather handsome. They had interviewed several additional people that had been at the concert but did not come up with anything.

The second young lady had gone out hiking along the country roads that were around her farm but never returned home. He had his men follow several hiking routes her mother described but again there was no additional evidence. He had driven each potential road that the young woman might have hiked and had not seen anything.

The third had gone to a night club where she often went, and she was last seen leaving as she chatted with a person that one of the waitresses said was a slender dark haired rather good-looking guy. She had looked out the window as the two got into a black pickup truck.

When she was asked about a license plate number, she said that she had no clue, but she did comment about the license plate holder. She described it as bright silver with red devil horns on each corner. He had his men look for black trucks, but none had that type of license plate holder.

Alex felt a shiver go down her back. She asked if the sheriff had the names of the friends and of the waitress. She also asked if he knew the hiking path that the other young woman had taken.

He said that he had the names, but he had no knowledge of the exact hiking path that the young lady had taken. He had walked out to the first country road with that young lady's mother but even the mother was not sure which way she would have gone because there were several more crossroads that she may have chosen to go down.

He added that he had one of his units travel every road looking for any clues but after a week they had come up empty.

Alex nodded and added that it was most likely that she had been whisked away and was not to be found.

She looked at Johnnie and asked if he had any additional questions or information.

Johnnie nodded and said that he had only enough time to search Hamilton County and Warren County records. He said that he had two more counties in Ohio and then counties in Indiana and Kentucky to search. He said that so far, he had six additional missing person reports that met her search criteria. He speculated that the number could double.

Alex nodded and let everyone know that she would go back and see if her boss would let her take on the case. She added that it appeared to her that a serial killer was at work.

Sheriff Milster asked why she thought it was a serial killer.

She shook her head and said that it was just a premonition.

She then asked Johnnie to shut down his search and they would go back to the office and once the case was officially agreed to, they would dig deeper and see if they could find who was doing the killing.

Both Sheriffs thanked her for coming out and listening to them and asked that they be contacted if the case was going to be taken up.

Alex said that she would of course do that. She then suggested that they give her Chief a call and request that he support making this an official case.

Sheriff Milster shook her hand and said that he was already feeling better and hoped that she would take on the case.

Once they were in the car Alex asked Johnnie how far back in time he had gone in his search.

Johnnie responded with the fact he had only searched back one year.

Alex asked him to do what he had done in the Pool of Blood case and determine when the serial killer had started his journey. She was not sure how long he had been at work but most likely his early years of his killing habit would have been at a low level.

Recent events may have triggered an increase in his activities. She asked Johnnie to identify the first victim and to chart out the hockey stick pattern she was expecting to see.

When they arrived at the station, Alex led the way to the Chief's office.

The Chief's door was open, and he waved her in. He asked whether he should call Bill and Trevor in.

Alex nodded and said that if he accepted the case she was about to describe, the case might cover the tri-state area and that would require a significant amount of coordination that would require their help.

The call from Loveland from the two sheriffs had prepared him and he had already alerted Bill and Trevor. He stepped to the door and signaled for them to come to his office.

Once everyone was in, he closed the door and asked Alex to fill them in on what she had learned over lunch with the two sheriffs. He shared the fact that both of them had talked to him and asked that he take up the case.

Alex positioned her chair so she could face the rest. She then took them through the details of the case and made the point that Johnnie had already surfaced six additional missing person reports that fit the description of the three missing person reports that Sheriff Milster had given them. She was relatively sure they were dealing with a serial killer who lived somewhere in the area and had recently increased his kill rate.

Bill asked why she thought the killing rate had gone up.

Alex replied that Johnnie had only gone back one year in his initial search and the number seemed high not to have been noticed earlier.

She had asked Johnnie to go back as far as possible to determine what the killing hockey stick data looked like. She commented that this was the approach that had helped her solve the case where she had dealt with a serial killer in Hawaii.

She added that she had promised Johnnie a tray of oatmeal raisin cookies for him to define the hockey stick for this case.

Trevor asked what he had to do to get a tray of her cookies.

Alex smiled and replied that Johnnie was checking the missing person reports in Hamilton County and all the surrounding counties and that they would need to interface with the seven counties that surrounded Cincinnati. She would like him and Bill to be the face of the team to each of the organizations involved and get them to give the team legal access to their missing persons reports.

Trevor gave a groan and asked why Johnnie got the easy work and he and Bill got the hard stuff.

Alex smiled and said that to make the deal a little sweeter she would add a tray of brownies to the deal. She added that this case gave him a chance to be in the news and she was doing this because she wanted to flaunt his superior capabilities.

Bill smiled and added that he knew that it was because, "she loved them too."

Alex smiled and said that the only person not getting any cookies promised to him was Trey, but she planned to bring a batch over to his house as soon as she received his next invitation to a back yard cook out.

The Chief spoke up and said that he was officially launching the investigation into a potential serial killer, and he would let the hierarchy know. He wanted it all kept low key until they were close to capturing the killer.

He did not want the news speculating on a potential serial killer operating in the Cincinnati area.

Alex said that she agreed to keep it low key and that the only other person in the department that she wanted to read in was Dr. Rogers. She figured his help would be critical if they found any bodies.

The Chief called the meeting to an end and suggested that the five of them figure out how to attack the case.

Alex led the way out of the office. She suggested that they spend the rest of the afternoon outlining how they would handle the case and what each of them would do. Then they could reconvene in the morning and set up a detailed plan.

Johnnie said that would give him some time to decide how to best reapply his Hawaii data search technique. He shared that he had learned a ton about programing in both the legal side and on the hacking side since then and thought he might be able to speed up the search.

Alex said that she was counting on him being able to give the team a way to identify this mysterious young man who drove a black pickup with red horns on the rear license plate holder.

3 Reconnection

*L*evi looked out of the windows of the third floor and took in the view of downtown Cincinnati and the Kentucky hills beyond. The river was mostly hidden but the tops of the bridges all were visible. The purple people's bridge reminded him of the walks he enjoyed taking across to the shopping center on the other side where he often took in a movie and afterwards, he would stop for a drink and then walk back to his house.

He really enjoyed working in his preparation room. It had been one of the major reasons he had purchased the house. The view had been one reason, but he also liked the way the third floor was arranged. He had recognized how the floor could be laid out like a cultural museum. He had spent a great deal of time thinking through the layout, the lighting, the floor details and even what would go on the fireplace mantles that each room had. He had no plans in using any of the fireplaces, he figured he would put some of his mother's nick knacks on the mantles.

He had all the carpeting ripped out and had the hardwood floor redone. On the third floor he had decorative stars put into the floor on which he would put his display stands that he had designed.

He also had the spot lighting installed. He was able to turn each light on and off separately at a control board at the entrance to each room. This let him stand at the entrance and highlight each skull independently. He often enjoyed going light by light slowly around the room. He would leave the room dark and turn on one light on the selected skull and then walk over and stand and admire it.

He had found a woodworking shop that made the pedestals that now was on each star. He had enough pedestals and stars to hold fifty heads. He figured he had enough space to double the size of his collection in the near future. He figured that might happen if he lived beyond eighty.

He had just finished putting the latest head on her pedestal. He felt that he was getting to be a top-level professional skull preparer. It took him a week of concentrated work to get the skull a nice white color. He had worked on perfecting the way he would slowly get the skull to be a translucent white color.

He would then carefully mount the skull on its brass holder. The brass holder was a bracket that he had designed and then had a small local company produce it. He had fifty of them, but he figured when he used all of them, he could go back and get more made.

He had thought through on how to increase his skull collection without alerting the police. He had decided to expand his search area across the tri-states and potentially randomly go even farther out. He identified all the state parks in the tristate area and researched when they had crowd gathering events.

The house was much too large for him, but he spent much of his time on the third floor with his collection, so it really did not matter to him. He had hired a house cleaning team that took care of the two first floors.

He enjoyed sitting on the couch near the window of the third-floor workshop as he spent time finding out about other events that gathered large crowds.

Outdoor venues like concerts were the best ones and when it got cold then there were outdoor venues like ice skating and skiing that were also quite good.

The indoor venues were a little more difficult to get to meet and lure one of his prizes, but he found that standing outdoors and observing the young women coming alone also yielded potential skulls.

He hung up a huge calendar in the third-floor work room that had all the events across the three states and then he prioritized which ones he planned to attend. He thought about the twenty five percent success rate that a hunting lion experienced when it hunted and figured that he didn't need to be that successful to keep his plate full.

He studied his calendar and figured that he had a solid ten days per month of event attendance. If he had a lion's success, he should easily be able to garner two heads a month. This represented a perfect fit with the time to properly process and put a head on display. He hoped it would also be low enough that the various agencies would not recognize what he was doing.

He smiled as he thought about the fun, he had with each of his conquests. He always treated them to as good a time as he could get them to accept. It was like giving the condemned their last meal before walking them to the gas chamber. He grinned and shook his head as he thought that the only difference was that he used chloroform as the gas that took them out.

He thought about how hard it had been to keep his personal hobby from his parents. They had both died one after the other. His dad went first and was followed by his mother less than a year later. He missed both of them, but his life had become much easier since they had passed away. He now had a home that his inheritance from them had made possible, where an entire floor was dedicated to what he considered his purpose in life.

It was so much more relaxing since he did not have to sneak around as he went about adding to his collection and he had been able to make his collection into a showcase that he could enjoy on a daily basis.

Levi had several restaurants in the Cincinnati area that he frequented fairly often. He was always on the lookout for his next head, but he made a point of only looking when he dined out while he focused himself in enjoying some unique dinner. But as his father use to say, "he looked at good looking women because he was not blind."

He was now very selective about where he was hunting because he had to drive to Cleveland to deliver his prizes. Because of that drive he had decided to extent the search area from Cincinnati to the Cleveland area. This would add new territory and distribute his take across additional different jurisdictions.

Columbus was the home of The Ohio State University. He bought football tickets offered by the scalpers and started to attend the games. Hunting there was relatively easy. There seemed to be an overabundance of beautiful young skulls. He was hesitant to harvest at the University but there was also a minor league ball club, many other events in downtown Columbus and a significant bicycle path that offered good hunting.

Cleveland had a professional football team that offered a hunting ground, but most single desirable heads could not afford to go to the games, but the surrounding nightclubs teamed with younger women interested in meeting someone and he was quite willing to be met.

He researched the events in both cities and added them to his calendar. He decided to try to get a head from each city every other month.

He set things up so that his next collection would be after a baseball game in Cleveland. He figured that the watering holes would provide the prey. He made the point of doing the rounds before the game to scope out the different bars and decided on the one he would go to during the next game.

He would focus on the game and on scoping out the potential new head. He felt good about his hunting ability. He would watch the single women and figure out which ones seemed to be on the hunt and who were not professionals. The professionals gave themselves away by being more aggressive in their hunt whereas the women that he was seeking were often more hesitant and sat at a table versus the bar.

When he approached the one, he had selected, he was lucky. She had a great smile and said she would love to dance when he asked. After the dance he asked if he could join her at her table. He learned her name was Madeline and she was attending nursing school. He and Madeline spent the evening talking and dancing. He invited her to dinner and again she accepted. He asked her to choose the restaurant and made sure she understood that a top end restaurant was fine with him.

She asked if it was alright to try Luigi's Steak Restaurant that had a five-star rating and was rather expensive.

He smiled as he said it seemed like a great choice and at the same time, he was thinking about it being her last meal and he wanted her to enjoy that.

The service and the dinner were superb. It was clear that Madeline was enjoying her meal.

Levi figured she would not have been so jubilant had she known it was to be her last meal.

He smiled to himself when later she accepted coming up to his room. He figured if she ate breakfast, she had one more meal coming. He would try to make sure it was one that she loved.

Once in his hotel room, he opened a bottle of his favorite wine that they shared. Madeline was enjoyable to talk to and to listen to the stories she shared about her younger years.

A short time later they went to the bedroom where he enjoyed a wonderful session of love making. He decided he would need to put this approach into use more often.

The next morning before breakfast he made a call to the processing center to let them know that he had a delivery on the way. He was assured that they would be ready.

Early the next morning he and Madeline went to Luke's breakfast place where Madeline ordered two eggs over easy, hush puppies, bacon, and a cup of coffee. She was in a jubilant mood and smiled and chatted away as she ate.

They got back to the truck and Levi asked for instructions to take her home.

Madeline never knew what hit her when he reached over and sprayed her with his chloroform spray. She went out like a light. He then opened both windows and let out the breath he was holding.

The chloroform spray was something that he had perfected and that made it so easy to overpower his victim.

He drove slowly to the body parts house and drove down the alley between the house on the corner and the smaller house across from it.

Three attendants came out and took Madeline in. The youngest of the three escorted him to the room on the second floor. He entered and was greeted by the person he only knew as Reston. He declined an alcoholic drink but accepted an iced tea.

He and Reston exchanged small talk. Reston periodically looked at a large screen that displayed the action taking place on the dissection table.

Reston said that it was a good body and placed fifty thousand dollars of cash out in bundles on his desk.

Levi thanked him and put the fifty bundles into the cloth bag that he had brought with him.

Reston stood up and let him know that the head was in the cooler by the door and said he looked forward to his next delivery.

Levi held up his bag, thanked Reston, and made his way out of the office. He was not sure he trusted Reston but the money he was getting for the bodies covered his worries. He was able to live a great life with the money that the bodies provided and he was slowly accumulating a huge nest egg.

He carried the cooler out to his truck and put it into his truck's built in toolbox. He dropped the bag of cash next to it and locked the toolbox.

He remembered the speeding ticket he had received recently and drove carefully to the highway and took his time driving just below the speed limit back to his house in Cincinnati.

He kept thinking about what a good time he and Madeline had shared and knew that she would be one of the special skulls in his collection. He would put a little gold star on her plaque

4 On the Hunt

*T*he following morning, Alex asked Johnnie to set up his computer so he could share the information he was getting from the counties around Cincinnati.

She asked Bill and Travis to put in a request for the names of each County's missing persons list and ask them for access to their computers and for the names of the persons who handled missing person reports.

She looked back to Johnnie and asked him to continue to hack his way through all the systems, but they would use his information only as a guide. She wanted to move with as much speed as possible but to collect all the formal information in a way that would stand up in court.

She reminded the team that speed against the SLATE groups had in each situation saved a young woman's life and she felt that speed in this case would save some women's lives.

Trevor nodded in agreement and said that it made him recall the fact in every battle she had been the first one in and the last one out. Her preparation had saved all of them.

He was all in on executing with speed. He just hoped that he would not end up with all the bullet hits he had taken in the last few cases.

Alex commented that she did not think this case would be one of gun battles but one that tested the speed of their thinking. She said that the Hawaiian serial killer was a loner, the Canadian was a loner and she figured that the one they were now after would be a loner.

Trey spoke up and said that he thought they were dealing with a persuasive loner but one that had a very troubled mind and was most likely capable of any action. He commented that serial killers were killers and when cornered they would react violently.

Johnnie displayed the telephone numbers for each surrounding county. He said that he had sent the numbers to each of the team's phones.

Bill took out his phone and confirmed that he had the numbers. He asked if it made more sense for him and Trevor to go to another room and begin the calling and arranging for the one-on-one visits for the two of them.

Alex nodded and said that was a good idea.

She looked at Johnnie and asked if he had the records of the bodies that had been found in Cleveland.

Johnnie said that he did.

She asked him to send them down to Dr. Rogers. She said that she was going down to the morgue and enroll him in the case.

Johnnie let her know the Dr. Rogers already had the paperwork from Cleveland. He would send him the missing person reports.

She asked Trey if he wanted to go with her to the morgue.

He smiled and said that he couldn't decline since she had just invited him to one of his favorite places to visit. Then he added, "not."

Dr. Slivers looked up from his desk as Alex walked in and commented that she looked like she was bringing work with her.

Alex smiled and said that indeed she was coming to ask for his help on a new case.

She briefly explained that there was an uptick on reports of missing young women, and she wanted to see if any of these missing women might be in the body parts collection that had been amassed in his morgue or in the Cleveland police morgue. She added that all the missing person reports had been sent to him and wondered if he could use that information to check against the female body parts.

Dr. Silvers replied that he indeed could as long as the missing person reports had DNA information.

Alex said she was not sure, but she would make sure that for every report, her team would obtain a DNA sample to go with it. She added that his work needed to be kept out of the general police information system and should not be made public.

Dr. Silvers smiled and replied that only she was the only person who spoke to him on a regular basis so it would be no problem.

Alex nodded and said that she only visited because he was her favorite department coroner.

"Ok, I am on the case and will make sure I keep you updated as I learn something," he finished and added that he was the only coroner in the department.

Alex smiled, nodded, and thanked him and walked out to the elevator.

Trey commented that he thought she had made the doctors day.

Alex said that he was the one that would most likely provide the material they would need to nail the person who was kidnapping and most likely killing young women.

If this person was delivering bodies to the body parts production system, then perhaps they might get a clue from when and where the bodies were being delivered.

Trey looked at her and said that he was getting the vibe that they would be talking to Dario once again.

Ale smiled and nodded that she had been wondering whether there might be a way to get Dario to shed some light on the case.

She wondered what Lindsey would think about the two of them taking a road trip to Cleveland or where Dario was now being incarcerated.

Trey suggested that she and Matt come over on Sunday around twelve for some grilled dogs and she could ask Lindsey that question.

Alex smiled and said that she had worked all morning to get an invite. She was not sure about Matt, but she would be over. She said that if Matt did not have duty he would also love to come. He always enjoyed playing with Nolan.

He said that it was almost quitting time and he figured he would go, change, go home and start the weekend. He wished her a safe ride back to her apartment.

He walked back with her to the team room and extended the invitation of a grill out in his back yard to the other team members.

He got a yes from Johnnie and declines from Bill and Trevor because they had fishing reservations down at Lake Cumberland. They said they would be glad to share part of their catch since they each planned to catch the limit which would be more than they could possibly handle.

Both Johnnie and Trey said they would love to get a fish or two.

Alex said that she would love to get a fish and then declared an end to the day and said she was going to change and ride back to her apartment.

Johnnie said he was ready.

On the way he asked what her plans were for the evening and for Saturday.

Alex said that she had none for the evening because Matt was on the second shift. The two of them were on for an early morning ride at sunrise and then Matt and she would have lunch but then he was once again off to work.

When they got to the apartment, Johnnie asked whether she was up for an early dinner that evening at their favorite Thai restaurant.

Alex said that sounded great, but she was going to do a few miles on the treadmill, take a quick shower and then she was ready for the walk over to the restaurant.

Johnnie replied that it sounded like a plan. He went into his apartment and got his computer online and then went and took a quick shower. A short time later, he walked down the hallway to the gym and looked in. Alex was still running full speed on an inclined treadmill. He shook his head and went back to his apartment and sat down and continued processing missing person reports.

He had been able to hack into all the counties that surrounded Hamilton County and had set up an automated search program that flagged the reports that Alex had specified.

He then set up a search going back ten years. He set up an algorithm to flag when a specific set of missing person reports took a hockey stick turn upwards.

He planned to leave his computer running the algorithms while he and Alex went to dinner. He figured when he got back, he would have the data from all the counties and then he could determine if there was a hockey curve set of data.

He spent the last few moments before he expected Alex to knock on his door setting up an integration routine that would combine all the missing person reports and again look for the hockey stick pattern in the combined data.

As he was finishing coding the routine, Alex's the familiar shave and a haircut knock was at his door.

He smiled and went to the door. He was looking forward to dinner and he hoped that afterward he could surprise Alex with the information that he hoped to have.

Alex sensed Johnnie's upbeat mood and asked what he had cooking.

Johnnie smiled and said that he had an after-dinner surprise for her that would be worth multiple trays of her cookies.

Alex knew better than to press for more, but she said that she wanted to have dessert at his place.

After what they both agreed had been a superb dinner, Johnnie set a brisk pace back to the apartment. He was eager to see what his database withdrawal routines had come up with. He knew that the hockey stick routine would define if the missing person pattern was limited to one county. He had set up the integration routine because he did not expect the missing person pattern to be limited to one county.

He was betting on it being a multicounty situation because three of the initial missing person reports were from Warren County and several seemed to be from Hamilton County.

He was expecting to fire off his integration engine against all the counties missing person reports to learn if a multicounty hockey stick curve would occur.

Alex was eager to get to Johnnie's apartment to learn what he was up to.

When Johnnie walked into his apartment, he took a quick look at his computer and smiled. He had the data from all the counties. He had the ingredients that with a little tweaking would present a breakthrough in the case. He set off his multi-county integration routine but left the graphing routine off because he wanted to have Alex launch it.

He went about leisurely serving dessert.

It was hard for Alex to relax as Johnnie made a production of getting out the ice cream and warming up some of the cookies she had brought down to him the day before.

It was clear to her that Johnnie was planning some sort of surprise for her. She took her first bite of ice cream and asked what he was so secretive about.

Johnnie replied that he had automated his search and now had all the missing person reports from all the surrounding counties.

He then explained that his routine had ruled out a hockey shaped curve for any one county but while they enjoyed desert, the routine was pulling all the information together and he was going to have her launch the graphing routine.

Alex complimented Johnnie on his ever-increasing programing expertise.

Johnnie nodded and said he had been working hard at improving not only his hacking capabilities but all his other coding skills. He commented that he had learned more about databases, their creation and management than he had ever dreamed about. He had investigated and reviewed the attributes of all the newer databases.

He smiled and added that the hacking field had also exploded and that both arenas seemed to be competing against each other.

He added with what he had learned, he had put many of his own twists to and then modified his hacking routines and had spent a great deal of time perfecting his ability to hack into a database and quickly set it up to voluntarily send out the information to an external non shielded program that he then collected and erased. This let him get the data and never be apprehended and made the trail to his hack virtually invisible.

Alex laughed at his explanation, said that she had a top-class pickpocket as her magician analyst and that she figured it was going to cost her many a cookie.

Johnnie checked to see if the integrating routine to was done. He made sure that the data was loaded into his hockey stick analyzer.

He turned the computer so Alex could see it and sat down next to her. He instructed her to hit the enter button.

Alex asked what she should expect when she hit enter.

Johnnie replied that she would see a hockey stick curve, the date of the first missing person report, and the counties that were involved with each subsequent missing person report.

Alex looked at him and asked if he was serious.

Johnnie nodded and reached over and pushed her finger down on the return button.

Alex smiled as the figure of a steel ball hitting a vertical one and to send it swinging up and returning to do the same to the ball that had hit it as the two marked time. She had a similar physical one on her desk at work and often spent time watching it when she was thinking. She figured Johnnie had used it on purpose.

Johnnie commented that this was his first time at using the data integration program and he was beginning to worry that there was a problem.

Then he let out a loud Marine "Hurrah" as the graph popped up and Hamilton and the three surrounding counties were on the list.

He pointed to the initial date and groaned.

Alex shook her head and asked if the hockey stick could possibly reach back twenty years.

Johnnie called up the missing person report for that date and the six subsequent ones. He said that even if the program was fifty percent off it would still reach back ten years.

Alex nodded as she silently went through what the team needed to do to verify what Johnnie had just presented. They would need to interview the people that had put in the missing person reports and if possible, get a DNA sample for each person. They would need to do that for every report that made up the curve.

It was monumental. She thought about her Pool of Blood case where they had concentrated on high schools and colleges around the location where the first missing person lived. She hoped that this first person would have been someone that was in the same school as the serial killer.

She looked at the detail of the first person and saw that she went to high school at a school in Warren County. This was the same county where Sheriff Milster had three recent missing person reports.

She gave Johnnie a hug.

He said that over the weekend he should do any additional tweaking he thought was necessary and that by Monday he would have every report available to share with the team.

She added that on Sunday they would share this with Trey when they went to the grill out at his place. On Monday they would bring the rest of the team on board.

She gave him another hug and said that he could pick any restaurant he desired to have lunch the next day, and it would be her treat.

Johnny sat back in his chair with what he knew was a huge smile. He felt great about the speed at which he had been able to come up with the information that he was certain would solve the case. He was personally proud of how far he had come since being saved by Alex.

He replied that he wanted to go to his favorite Brazilian churrascaria. He suggested they walk so he could have a few of his favorite Caipirinha drinks.

Alex nodded and said that she hoped they could do that drink without alcohol so that she could join him.

She looked at the time and said that it was time for her to get to bed so she could get up in the morning and get a bike ride in with Matt.

5 Closing In

*J*ohnnie could not put down the top of his laptop. He kept processing and analyzing. He spent all of Saturday morning getting information on the first five victims. He identified their school and the years they had gone there. He needed some additional information to get things to fit together.

He hit upon it when the fourth missing person report was in a high school in the same area that was in Sheriff Milster's jurisdiction. He got into the school's computer but was disappointed that they had not transferred their old records into it but had chosen to only put the information in since the installation of the new computer system.

He was at least pleased that Bill and Travis would be able to go to the school and get the yearbooks so they could search through them for their serial killer. He knew that Alex would work her way through all the likely young men in the yearbook. Like her previous case she would be like a coon dog on the trail and would not stop until she had the rascal treed and was baying at the moon.

He gave a small laugh thinking about his comparing her to an old coon dog. He thought about it again and decided she was more like an attacking Rottweiler or a ferocious Doberman, a force to be reckoned with and deadly.

He closed his laptop and looked at the time. It was just twelve and he had a great lunch to look forward to.

He decided to wait for Alex by the elevator. He had no more gotten there than Alex walked out with a great smile on her face.

She let him know that she had called ahead, they had a reservation and she had been assured that the bar tender would make her a caipirinha with no alcohol.

The two of them set a leisurely pace and a short time later arrived at the restaurant and were shown to their table. They put in their drink order and were just toasting with their first drink when a young girl came to the table and asked for her autograph.

Alex looked around and was waved to from a table across the room. She asked the girl's name and then signed her name and put in one of her favorite sayings, "dream your dream, then act to make it real."

Johnnie watched the interaction, and he modified his previous description to a Doberman with a loving heart.

He had joined Alex in ordering an alcoholic free caipirinha and commented that he would most likely just get a sugar high, but he liked it better than the alcoholic version.

Alex said that she liked the fact that the bartender had so easily matched the flavor of a real one. She said that she was going to help herself to the palm heart, caviar, and olives from the salad bar before all the meat began to arrive.

Johnnie joined her but focused on the deviled eggs and the smoked fish that was also at the salad bar. He walked around it and decided a complete meal could be had just at the salad bar.

Alex returned to the table, enjoyed the palm hearts and the variety of meat that was piling up on her plate. She finally turned up the red side of her card to indicate she was done taking any more meat. She looked at what was on her plate and wondered if she would be able to eat it all.

The family with the young girl that had asked for her autograph came over and the mother thanked her for giving her autograph and for the inspirational message. She added that the family had followed her many cases and thought of her as a Cincinnati heroine.

Alex nodded and thanked her for her kind comments, and she wished her daughter great success in school and college beyond high school.

After the family left Alex looked at Johnnie and commented that she would like the incident kept out of the office.

Johnnie looked at her and replied that she was just a shy Doberman with a warm heart.

Alex had no idea what he was referring to and she focused on the various pieces of meat still on her plate.

After they had finished, she said she was going to walk to the river and then along the river front wall to the symphony in the park greens and then back to the apartment. She asked if he wanted to walk along with her.

Johnnie readily agreed.

As they walked, he shared what he had learned where it had all started and that he thought he had the high school where the first victim had attended but verification would require old-fashioned footwork because the records were in paper form.

Alex responded that he had been holding back on her.

Johnnie gave a small laugh and said that he had done so because he wanted to enjoy lunch without talking about work related stuff.

Alex said that she would have him share his breakthrough with Trey and with the Chief if he was at the picnic.

Johnnie agreed and said that they should make sure that they did not scare the kids.

Alex nodded and said she would make sure the kids were either across the yard or playing inside.

The walk was just what she needed. When she was back in the apartment, she let Johnnie know that she was going to put as much time as possible in the gym, take a shower, read a good book, and then get to bed early.

Johnnie asked what time Matt got off his EMT shift.

Alex said that it would be something like three in the morning.

Johnnie let out a groan and commented that he didn't know how Matt kept the pace that he did.

Sunday morning Alex focused on baking cookies and making chocolate fudge with her mix of nuts, wedges of figs and diced marshmallow.

Matt came out from the bedroom and complained it was impossible to sleep when she baked. He poured himself a cup of coffee and volunteered to be a taste tester.

Alex apologized for disturbing his sleep and gave him a square of fudge and an oatmeal cookie. She asked him if he wanted something more substantial.

Matt shook his head and said that he was going to save his stomach for whatever Lindsay and Trey had for their grill out.

He asked her how her lunch with Johnnie had gone.

Alex shared that lunch was great but even better was the breakthrough that Johnnie had made on the case. She said that she would save that for Johnnie to share during the grill out.

Matt went to the couch and stretched out.

Alex smiled when she saw that he was sleeping.

She prepared a tray of cookies and fudge and took it down to Johnnie's apartment.

She had a cup of coffee with him and asked what he had been up to.

Johnnie replied that he had been able to process all the missing persons reports and had gotten all the addresses listed so that they could be assigned to anyone doing the investigation.

He had wondered if the two sheriffs would be willing to assign resources to make initial contact with the families of the missing women.

Alex said that she thought that was a great idea since they would be closer to the area and more likely to be known to the people then someone from Cincinnati.

She let Johnnie know that she was planning to leave for Trey's house around eleven because she wanted to get there early.

When she returned to the apartment, she saw that Matt was still asleep on the couch. She decided to change into her gym outfit and go work out at the gym.

Matt woke up and saw the sticky note on the edge of the couch cushion. It said, "at the gym." He looked at the time and decided to take a hot shower.

Alex came in from the gym and heard the shower. She smiled and walked into the bathroom stripped, opened the shower door, and asked if she could join in.

Matt smiled and pulled her in. He made sure the shower stall became even steamier.

After the shower he dried Alex off and luxuriated as she returned the favor.

A short time later Alex led the way to her car.

Johnnie met the two as they exited the elevator. He commented that he did not want to know why the two were smiling like Cheshire cats.

They all got into her car and drove to Trey's house. The entrance to the highway took her under the bridge where she, Trey and her assigned bodyguard had been attacked. She was hit several times, but her Kevlar vest had saved her. Her bodyguard had taken three hits to the chest but had also survived because she was wearing the vest that Alex had insisted, she wore. The shooters were not so lucky. Alex shot both in the neck just below their protective helmets and above the body armor they were wearing.

She shook her head as the thought went through her head.

A few moments later they arrived at Trey's home.

Lindsey greeted them at the door and Nolan ran out to Alex and gave her a hug as he shouted out, "it's Aunt Alex and her gang." He shook Johnnie's hand and then he gave Matt a hug and took his hand and said he had the Chess board set up and ready to go.

Alex smiled and followed Lindsey into the kitchen. She watched as Johnnie went out through the enclosed porch and out to where Trey stood at the grill.

Lindsey looked at Alex and asked what she was supposed to ask her about.

Alex smiled and said that originally, she was going to ask when the best time to go to Cleveland would be in the coming week but that had changed because the person she was planning to question had been transferred to the Mansfield Correctional Institute and that would be a day trip with an early departure and a late return if the questioning took more time than expected.

Lindsey smiled and replied that she didn't need to approve trips even if they took longer than expected. She knew that the team was always trying to get ahead of some killer before another person fell victim.

Alex nodded and replied that it haunted her when she realized that a day often meant the loss of another life.

Lindsey nodded and said that Trey also shared that view and praised the team at its willingness to put in the extra time and effort. He made the point that she had brought Bill and Trevor into the fold and had created an unbeatable team association.

Alex smiled and said that Trey was the rock that held the them together by the example he had displayed during the gun battles they had faced. She showed the picture of the gun Trey had been using that had a bullet in the barrel and had been shot out of his hand.

Lindsey smiled and said that was a picture she had on her nightstand that she often looked at before saying her nightly prayer. She was sure it represented a miracle.

Alex nodded and said that she would have too many pictures of what she called miracles if she tried to put them on a nightstand. She added that each picture was embedded in her mind, and she prayed all day long.

Lindsey suggested they go out to the porch and sit down with a glass of iced tea and wait for Trey to bring in his grilled prizes. She added that Trey had decided to focus on steak and was grilling Filet mignon, New York strip, Top sirloin, Ribeye and Steak tips and a variety of grilled veggies.

She had made a sliced tomato, cucumber salad with only olive oil drizzled over it. She figured that each person could salt and pepper it to their taste.

Alex commented that it all sounded great.

Lindsey replied that it was an easy way to make a filling lunch for a large group.

Alex asked who would be coming.

Lindsey replied that Annie and the girls were on the way and that the Chief, and his wife were on the way as well. They had received, "a have a good time from both Bill and Trevor" saying that the fishing was really great, and they would bring some of their catch back to share.

Alex said she looked forward to having Annie come over because she always enjoyed watching Laurie and Linda playing with Nolan.

Lindsey nodded and said the three were the best of friends and they were always talking about the highlights of the cases that Trey had with the team.

Alex smiled and said that she would need to emphasize the need to go to college to be able to do what one loved doing.

Lindsey smile and commented that Trey had shared that she was worried about being thought of as a gunslinger. She went on to say that she should not worry because she had listened as the three kids talked about all the skills that their, "Cincinnati Black Annie Oakley" had beyond just being the best shot in the world she was the smartest, the best at flying a hover craft, the best in hand-to-hand combat, the best at throwing a knife or a hatched. She laughed and said the list went on as each tried to outdo the other at what their favorite "Aunt" was best at.

Alex smiled and said that she should be thankful that she had the reputation of being the best.

Just then the front doorbell rang, and Alex jumped up and reached for the weapon that was not on her but locked in the car glove compartment.

Lindsey noticed and put her hand on Alex's and said she knew it was Annie and got up as Annie walked onto the porch carrying a foil covered tray that she put on the serving table.

She came over and gave both Lindsey and Alex a hug.

Alex got down on her knees to hug Linda and Laurie and laughed when she realized that the two were now taller than she was if she kneeled. She got up and finished the hug and asked when they had grown so much and that it was only a couple of weeks ago that they had been at the pool and were little.

Annie replied that it was a little over a month ago, but she agreed that the two had shot up dramatically during that month.

The doorbell rang again, and Lindsey went out and let the Chief and his wife in.

Trey and Johnnie each carrying a foil covered tray came in and put the grilled meat down and came over and joined in welcoming everyone.

Lindsey called down into the basement for everyone to come up and get their food. She then asked for some help in bringing out the salad and the drinks.

As she walked by the end of the table, she flipped open the cooler that had a variety of soft drinks and several visible bottles of Pelligrino.

Alex took in the gathering and knew that she was lucky to be in a job that had a great boss and such great and loyal friends.

Matt looked at the time and commented that his team had exchanged positions with another EMT team and had the north part of the county as coverage. This gave him a couple more hours but then he would have to leave.

Nolan said that would be enough time for them to finish their Chess game.

Matt smiled and said it was clear he was on the way to losing so they should play a game where Linda and Lauri could join in and the three of them could figure out how to beat him.

Alex was always surprised at how well Matt interfaced with the three kids. She figured he was going to be a good father.

She decided to take a couple of bites of each meat, several pieces of grilled vegies and the salad with a bottle of Pelligrino and when she looked at her plate, she knew that it was all that she could possibly eat.

She noted that everyone had dug in and was busy eating and talk fell almost to silence except for the praise for how good the food was.

Matt and the kids were the first to get done and they headed for the basement.

When Lindsey, Annie and Rose-Anne went to the kitchen to clean things up Alex went to the top of the basement stairs and let Matt know it was time for him to join everyone on the porch.

Lindsey went down to play with the kids.

Once Matt was seated Alex asked Johnnie to share what he had learned and the additional focus he was able to provide that would accelerate the team in solving the case.

The Chief shook his head and asked if any of the information could be used in court.

Alex shook her head in the negative and said that Bill, Trevor, she, and Trey would use the breakthrough that Johnnie was providing to gather the evidence needed in court to send whoever the serial killer happened to be to jail and that he should stand by to announce the success of the case to the public.

The Chief nodded and said that sounded like a good plan, but they should figure out what the public message should be. Even if the case was solved, he did not want to go in front of the news with the fact that a twenty-year-old serial killing case had been solved.

Rose-Anne came out and asked whether the three of them in the kitchen had given them enough time because it was time for either tea or coffee and dessert.

Alex nodded and said that Monday was the next time the team would focus on getting on with solving the case and that dessert definitely took precedence over work.

6 Shoe Leather Patrol

*M*att had been picked up by his team and when the grill out ended, Alex left with Johnnie, but stayed off the highway. She asked if it was OK to take her time because she wanted to think about the case and how they might speed it along.

Johnnie said he had no need to rush home. He said that they should start with the high school where the first girl had come up missing. He pointed out that it was going to take a very personal tone when they approached the persons who had put in the missing person reports, and they should make sure that Sheriff Milster took the lead but that they go with him to each place.

Alex nodded and she said that Bill and Trevor should go to the high school and get into the yearbook and other paper documents that they identified as pertinent. She added that the Sheriff should do the initial introduction to the high school staff to ensure their cooperation and help.

Johnnie suggested that they bring on board a couple of the Sheriff's deputies to aid in any follow-up that might be needed that the team didn't have time for.

Alex turned into the police station parking lot and parked in the back of the lot farthest from the door. She snickered and commented that no one ever parked in her personal parking spot.

She then locked the car and led the way toward their apartment building. On the way she asked whether Johnnie had been able to retrieve his bicycle from the police evidence lot.

He replied that he had forgotten to follow up but had expected to get notification when it was no longer considered evidence.

Alex nodded and said that she too had forgotten since they both were riding their second set of bikes, but they should follow up the next day.

They arrived at the apartment building and parted ways at the elevator.

Alex had enjoyed the day and decided to take a shower, relax with a cup of tea and a good book.

She figured the week ahead would be a long and tough one. She planned to go and question Dario to see if there was any connection between the body parts factory and the serial killer she was now hunting. She would have Bob and Trevor get the information from the high school and arrange an interview with the parents of the missing persons that she had in mind.

She wanted Trey and her to do the interviews, but she also wanted Sheriff Milster to be present.

She decided that she needed to spend the next morning making sure the team was organized and coordinated. She wanted everything to move rapidly and lead to the capture of the serial killer.

The next morning Johnnie met Alex at the elevator said hello and said she needed to put on her headset so he could get her up to date on what he had been finding out about their serial killer.

Alex could tell that Johnnie had pulled another one of his all-night hunting sessions. She listened as he talked all the way into work. She cringed when he said that the hockey stick that begun some fifteen years ago had a steep slope before reaching the point where it went asymptotic.

She asked how many missing women made up the hockey stick.

Johnnie replied that he estimated that there might be as many as forty.

Alex almost fell off her bike. She exclaimed, "Forty, how could forty missing person reports not raise a red flag."

Johnnie replied that the reports were scattered over time across seven counties and three states. He said that to this date the different organizations did not have a unified database. He had hacked into more than one database per county. He added that getting the official paperwork from each office would keep Bob and Trevor fully occupied for more than a week.

Alex got off her bike and rolled it through the door and told Johnnie that he should set up in the team room and she would get the rest of the team to join him. She went to locker room where she was now keeping her bike. She changed to her work clothes and went to the bullpen area where the only other persons that had arrived were Bill and Travis.

Bill said good morning and pointed to the box of donuts.

Alex smiled and said they should all grab a cup of coffee and go to the huddle room where she hoped Johnnie had already set up his computer.

She was leading the way to the huddle room when Trey came in with his cup of coffee and followed them.

Once in the room she said that they needed to accelerate in what they were doing because Johnnie had spent all night hacking and had determined that the serial killer was possibly killing up to four women a week.

Trevor shook his head. He commented that seemed high and that it would have sent up red flags.

Alex said she agreed with him, but the serial killer had been strategic about his killing by spreading his hunt across more than seven counties. She pointed out that even if Johnnie was fifty percent wrong it would still be twenty-four women per year at the current hockey stick curve rate.

Trey sighed and commented that so far Johnnie had delivered. He was shocked at the number but said that the team should not spend time arguing about the number but get clear what each of them had to do to get the killer ASAP.

Alex nodded. She then asked Bill and Trevor to do three things. First arrange to interview the parents of the first missing person and of the three missing persons that Sheriff Milster had given them.

Second get the high school yearbooks for the time the first missing woman was in high school.

And finally collect all the official missing person reports that Johnnie had identified. She asked that they gather the missing person reports in reverse time order and see if they could also get DNA samples with each of the reports.

Trevor laughed and asked if that was all he and Bob had to do.

Alex smiled and let him know that if he wore out the soles of his shoes, she would buy him a new pair. She then added that she planned to take it easy was going was letting Trey drive her to Mansfield where they would do one easy interview, have a luxurious lunch, and then drive back.

She pointed at Johnnie and said that she was sending him home to get some sleep because she wanted him to be awake when on Wednesday, she would interview the parents of the first missing person.

Then on Thursday she wanted to interview the parents of the three missing persons that Sheriff Milster had brought to them.

Bill spoke up and added that it was going to be a hell of a week and that the way she was pushing them she might solve the case by Friday.

Alex replied that she wished that would happen.

She then said that it was time for the team to split up and get to work. She was going to go to the morgue and enroll Dr. Rogers to check the body parts he had and the body parts in Cleveland to see if any of them matched the DNA of the missing women.

She looked at Trevor and asked him to send any DNA information that he gathered to Dr. Rogers.

Trevor smiled and asked if instead of a pair of new shoe he and Bill could get a tray of cookies.

Alex laughed and said that she would give him a tray of cookies next week for all the good work he did this week.

Bill laughed and asked if she were quoting from a Popeye cartoon.

Alex nodded and added that they should also believe that the cookies were in the mail. Then she said that it was time to get to work.

The Chief had arrived, and he saw Alex and Trevor exchanging a series of comments. He wondered what was up.

He watched as the team left the huddle room. It was clear that Johnnie was leaving. Bob and Trevor each went to their desks and got on their phones.

He waited as he watched Alex heading for his office.

He was shocked when she brought him up to date and what her plans were. He could not believe the number of potential victims that had been identified.

When he was asked to arrange for a late afternoon interview of Dario at the Mansfield Correctional institute he nodded and asked what time he should schedule the interview.

Alex looked at the time and said she had to stop at the morgue then they had about a two-hour drive. So, they would be there by eleven. She added that she wanted the interview to be with only the three of them.

The Chief nodded. He said that it would be against the normal procedure, but he would share the fact that they needed to protect their informant.

Alex thanked him and said that she would be back the same day unless they needed to do some other errand. She then led the way to the morgue.

Dr. Silver looked up from his desk and commented that it looked like more work had just walked in.

Alex nodded and said that the case needed acceleration and it needed him to deliver a breakthrough. She then brought him up to speed.

Dr. Silver bowed his head and said that if she had come to him with her story before he had gotten involved with processing the body parts in her last case, he would not have believed what she had just shared.

He said that he understood the need for speed. He would check the body parts against DNA from the missing person reports.

Alex thanked him and asked him to just put the information in her team folder.

She then excused herself and led the way out to the car.

Trey asked whether she needed to stop and buy some bags of chocolate.

Alex nodded and said that when they got to Mansfield, she also wanted to stop at a fast-food place and buy a full meal with a Strawberry swirl smoothie.

Trey smiled and said, "chocolate for the guards and a smoothie for Dario."

Alex nodded and said that she was a devoted follower of her mother's advice.

It was clear they were expected when they arrived at the correctional institute. They were guided to a specific parking spot and then led into the main office building where the institute director met them.

He introduced himself and said that he was familiar with her reputation and that her boss had emphasized the need to keep the information she was seeking from having any way to get out. He said that he would go with them to the interview room and make sure that they had total isolation.

He thanked her for the bag of chocolate Alex had given him and smiled. He asked how many more bags she had with her.

Alex replied that she had one bag for every officer that had been asked to step back. She lifted her bag that had a triple cheeseburger, fries, and the strawberry swirl. She said that the bag was her interview equipment.

The director nodded and said that he figured she would prevail and get the information she was after. He then asked her to follow him and led the way to the interrogation room.

Alex saw that Dario had his hands chained to the table. She asked that Dario's hand be freed and that his leg chain be secured to the ring.

When two guards came in to make that change, Alex asked how many of the guards had been asked to step back from their normal duties.

The older of the two said that there were four of them that were asked to do so.

Alex thanked them for their cooperation and handed them four bags of candy that they should share.

Both guards smiled and said that a chocolate reward would make them all enjoy the break from their normal routine.

The director pointed to the call button and said she should press it if they need anything and left with the two guards.

Alex looked at Dario and pushed the bag over to him. She said that she hoped that a triple cheeseburger and fries would help him to answer the questions she would be asking him but first she wanted to hear how he was doing at the institute.

Dario took out the smoothie and took a sip, then the burger and took a bite, he closed his eyes, and then replied that he wanted to thank her for putting his life on a path that he thought of as salvation.

He said that he was taking educational courses that would give him a high school equivalent degree and that since he was going to be in jail for most of his life, he planned to take college courses and get a degree. He added that he was thinking of getting a psychology equivalent degree and see how he could help inmates in the prison system.

He then smiled and said that he had fallen in love with raising and training dogs that then were provided to the community. He laughed and said that he trained them well so they could go out to the community and be free to enjoy their life.

He looked at Alex and thanked her for helping him get transferred to the institute.

Alex smiled and said that she hoped he would be able to find a useful way to spend his life. It would not be the same as being free but if he was lucky, it would be fulfilling.

She then said that she needed his help and that it dealt with the body production system.

She asked how the bodies were procured.

Dario was quiet for a moment. He then said that he was not sure how the specific bodies were procured but there were about a half dozen regular guys that brought the person in either alive or just recently killed.

They were on some sort of payment system where they brought the body in and then left immediately after delivery with an impressive amount of cash. He was not sure how much they got for a body, but his two partners said that it was fifty thousand dollars.

Alex asked if there were any other person or persons that were not the normal body parts providers.

Dario was silent for a moment as he took several bites of the burger and a sip of the smoothie. He then nodded and said there was one weird guy. He was rather good looking, and he brought in several women that were still alive but out. He would go up to the boss's office and wait for the only part of the body he wanted.

Dario shook his head and said the guy only wanted the skull.

Alex closed her eyes for a moment as she took in what Dario had said and the impact it had on the case. It added a horrific element that had not entered her mind until Dario shared the part of about the skull.

She then asked if Dario had ever seen the vehicle that this person drove.

Dario nodded. He said that it was a large black Dodge pickup that had a large built-in toolbox where this guy always put the cooler with the skull and a bag that he thought was probably full of money. He added that the guy was always polite and said thanks for the skull as if it was a normal thing.

Alex asked if he had ever seen the license plate number.

Dario closed his eyes for a significant amount of time and then said that what stood out was the shiny license plate holder with a red horn on each corner. He added that he thought it was a vanity plate because it was different than most cars. He could recall the letters LAM and that the numbers were two thousand something.

Alex asked if there was anything else that Dario might recall.

Dario said that the last delivery was different in the fact that the guy was humming a tune that reminded him of someone's song about having done it their way. It seemed that the guy was unusually happy.

Alex thanked Dario for his time. She asked if he had any request.

Dario smiled and said that if there was another interview, he would like to have Spaghetti De Mare with Alfredo sauce.

Alex replied that if his information was used to solve the case she was working on, she would have the meal delivered.

She then asked Trey to push the call button.

She waved to Dario as the four guards came in.

The director met them and walked with them to the car. He said that Dario represented somewhat of a mystery to him because he had been transferred to him with a sealed folder. He was a model prisoner and was thought of highly by the guards.

He asked why he had a life sentence.

Alex replied that he had lost his way in his previous life and had been associated with the worst of the worst. He had been instrumental in getting a very horrible case solved and she had worked to give him a second chance in life but a life behind bars.

The Director nodded and asked if he had provided her with the information she needed.

Alex said that she thought so and if he had she would like to reward him with a dinner he had expressed he would love to have.

The Director smiled and said that he hoped to arrange for that meal, and it would be in his office.

Alex asked him if he liked Spaghetti De Mare with Alfredo sauce.

The director nodded and said he hoped the information would help her solve the case.

Alex shook hands with him and led the way to the car.

Trey looked at her and asked if she thought she had gotten the information she needed.

Alex shook her head and said that she had gotten more than she had bargained for. Their serial killer was a skull collector. He was young, rather good looking and vain. He had vanity plates.

She said that it was going to be hard not to spend the night working with Johnnie to see if they could determine who the guy was.

She shook her head again and quietly added, "a serial killer who collected skulls."

She looked at Trey and said that if that didn't keep one up at night or in being scared to walk alone at night then there was nothing that would affect you

.

7 The Body Count

*I*t was hard for Alex to keep herself from calling the entire team together to share what she thought was a huge breakthrough. She decided to go to the gym and run on the treadmill until she was exhausted. Then she would think through how to adjust the team's effort based on what she knew.

As she ran, she came to realize that she really did not have anything concrete. She had no evidence, she had no criminal, she had nothing but some great leads. She was glad that the run had cleared her mind.

She wanted to get Johnnie to do some more digging but decided to wait until morning. As she got off the treadmill her phone gave the Matt ring. He said he was on the way back to the apartment and asked if he should pick up dinner. She told him to surprise her and get whatever he fancied. She said she was going to take a quick shower and would see him soon.

She was under the hot shower thinking about how to accelerate the case when the door to the shower opened and Matt asked if he could join her. Her thoughts about the case evaporated and she pulled him in.

They were both drying off when Matt's phone rang. It was the surprise meal delivery.

Alex asked if he had ordered drinks and got a no. She said she would make some iced tea while he went down to get the dinner.

Alex smiled when Matt let her know that is was Spaghetti Vongole. It was different from what she had promised Dario, but it was Italian. Matt had added Pan Fried Scamorza, Potato Focaccia rolls and a small mixed salad.

She figured that she was getting a message from above and was able to put her case away for the night.

She was up early the next morning and went down and knocked on Johnnie's door.

He let her in and offered a cup of coffee and breakfast if she wanted some.

Alex asked if he had caught up on his sleep.

Johnnie smiled and said that he had indeed. He had slept twelve hours and was eager to go after whatever she wanted.

She smiled and said that once they got to the office, she was going to inundate him with work but now she was going up fix breakfast for her and Matt and then she would be ready for their ride to work.

Johnnie said he could hardly wait.

Once they got to work, Alex called the team into the huddle room. She asked each person to give an update of what they had accomplished the previous day.

Bill highlighted the fact that they had contacted all the missing persons offices in every county of interest and had set up times to visit each to get the desired missing person reports.

Trevor said that he had worked with Sheriff Milster to set up the desired interviews. Two interviews would be on Wednesday and two would be on Thursday.

Alex said that what she was going to share would potentially change some of what the team would do. She then went through the information that Dario had provided.

She looked at Johnnie and asked him to locate the truck and the owner of the truck. Once he had that she wanted to know where he lived and his complete life history.

She looked at Bob and Trevor and said that she was not sure when but as soon as Johnnie identified the serial killer, they would then begin to shadow him. She was not sure for how long, but it would be until Johnnie provided them with what the perp owned and them getting search warrants. She expressed the fact that she wanted the team to put on their after burners and she wanted to capture the serial killer tomorrow.

Trevor shook his head up and down and said that once again Bob and he got the shaft and had to do the hard work.

Alex smiled and reminded him that he was about to get multiple trays of cookies.

"Cookies as the bribe to get me to smile," he said as he put up a fake smile.

Johnnie interrupted and said the he had the killer's name, address, and truck license plate number.

Alex looked at Bob and Trevor and said they would have to begin their tailing work sooner rather than later.

She added that she would get the Chief to assign a police unit to go and collect the missing person information from the various police precincts.

Trevor smiled and said that getting that chore reassigned was almost as good as a tray of cookies.

Bill asked if she cared how he and Trevor tailed the killer.

Alex shook her head and said anyway he wanted to as long as the killer had no clue.

He asked whether they could use her car during work hours. At night they would use their own cars. This would give them four cars to switch around and not be so obvious when they were following him.

Alex put her car keys on the table and said that they were available for them to use.

Johnnie spoke up and said that he had found the name of the person the that the house was registered in, and that this same person owned a farm.

Bob reminded Alex that the interviews were set for the next two days and for her not to miss them. He picked up the keys and walked out of the huddle room with Trevor following behind.

Trevor looked back, smiled, and said he preferred brownies.

Alex smiled. She felt the team kicking into action and the case coming to a thundering close. She could feel them making progress.

She said that it was time for them to update the Chief and get him to have search warrants prepared and the searches scheduled and staffed.

She wanted to proceed as fast as possible, but she wanted to have an airtight case. She wanted one that took the killer off the street permanently and maybe sent him to the gas chamber.

What bothered her was that she did not want a trial to expose the hideous nature of what happened to the missing young women. They were dead but their parents and close friends would be very negatively affected if they learned the details of the deaths of their loved ones.

Trey had been watching Alex and knew that she was up tight as ever. They had an AA meeting that evening and he was trying to figure out how he could help her release some of her tension.

Alex looked at Trey and said that she could read his mind and that no he should not try to question her at the AA meeting about what was bothering her. She said that she thought the killer had been looking for his prey during the concert that she and Matt had attended and that he had scoped her out.

Trey asked what had happened.

Alex said that Matt had gone and purchased an ice cream cone and tried to identify who was watching her. When he came back, he said that there seemed to be three guys toward the top of the lawn that were alone.

Trey nodded and said that was creepy.

Trey then said that maybe if they went to lunch with Johnnie, they could let him relieve their tension.

Alex said that sounded good and that the three of them should share what they had with the Chief. She said that afterwards they would go to the morgue to see if Dr. Rogers had anything for them.

She led the way to the Chief's office.

The Chief kept saying he didn't believe it, but he was glad to get warrants, arrange for the searches and get the missing person reports picked up. He said that the only condition that he was going to ask to be followed was that he, Trey, and she had to be at every location during the searches.

Alex nodded and said she would like to include Johnnie as well. She added that she wanted to keep Bill and Trevor following the killer.

The Chief nodded and said he would have search warrants that day.

Alex thanked him and left and went down to see Dr. Rogers in the morgue.

When she arrived and shared what she had learned about the case, he shook his head and said that he thought the body parts case was an extreme and now she had just taken that to an entirely weirder level.

She let him know that Johnnie would give him the forensic information about the missing women and that she wanted to know which ones were to be found in the body parts that were either in Cincinnati or in Cleveland.

Dr. Rogers nodded and said that he had all the information about the body parts in his computer system and he would identify any matches. He asked how many bodies their might be all together and when Johnnie shared that there might be forty or more women, he stopped for a moment and let the magnitude set in.

He asked how that would even be possible without it having been identified long ago.

Alex said that had been her question as well. She then pointed out that Johnnie had accessed seven different missing persons databases and there were probably some that had never made it into those systems.

She made the point that this serial killer was probably very cognizant of keeping a low profile by spreading a wide net.

She thanked him and then led the way back to her desk.

She got the addresses of both the house and the farm and said that she wanted to drive by the house and then drive out to the farm to get an idea of the logistics associated with the searches.

The drive to Mt. Adams to the house took only a few minutes.

The turret tower that rose one level to the third-floor roof line was the dominant feature of the mud-colored brick mansion looking home. She commented that their serial killer seemed to have all the money he needed. He not only had a huge home but also owned a six-hundred-acre farm in the middle of Ohio.

She suggested having lunch at one of the restaurants on Mt. Adams before driving to the farm.

The restaurant menu had a wide assortment to choose from. Alex decided on a large mixed salad and an iced tea. She took a bite of Trey's roast beef and a bite of Johnnie's T-bone steak.

Johnnie commented that he had brought along Gunjfor because the farmhouse was in the middle of a wooded area and at least a mile into a heavily wooded area at the back of the farm. He said that he could fly her in and allow them to see the area without trespassing.

Alex complimented him for thinking ahead.

She drove about an hour to get to the farm and parked at the side of the road and the three of them sat with their backs to the car.

Johnnie flew Gunjfor across the tall stalks of corn. He commented that there was a great yield of corn. He then crossed a green clover field that was almost ready to be mowed and baled. The arial view provided the perspective that highlighted the isolation of the farmhouse.

Johnnie hovered over the large brick farmhouse that had sometime in the past been modified and expanded more than once. There was a small road over grow with weeds that left the house and went back to a small lake that had a deck jutting out to where a large flatbottomed boat was tied. Johnnie quickly turned Gunjfor back over the trees when he spotted someone sitting on the deck fishing.

He zoomed the camera in and got a close up of the person's back.

Alex suggested they call it a day and leave. She said that she did not want to give their suspect any warning about being on the team's radar.

She asked Trey to drive because she wanted to make a couple of calls.

She called Bill to let him know that Levi Misle was at his farm fishing. She asked them if they could position themselves and begin their surveillance when he left the farm. She smiled when she heard Trevor complain about having to spend the night in the car.

She knew how she felt about such situations and suggested they a get good dinner and load up on snacks in case they did have to spend all night.

Johnnie suggested they bring one of their drones so they could keep track of Levi if he chose to stay on the farm.

Trevor replied that the drone would at least give him an opportunity to have some fun.

Alex wished them good luck and then called the Chief to find out what he had arranged.

The Chief was glad that Alex had called in. He let her know that the search warrants were issued and that he had scheduled the searches for Friday at noon. There would be two backup units at the house, two at the farm where they would work with Sheriff Milster and his team. They all knew to stand by until they got his orders. He said that the Sheriff was surprised by the address of the farm because he was acquainted with the family who had always been cordial to him and his officers.

Alex thanked the Chief and let him know that she and Trey would be with Sheriff Milster to interview the parents of the three victims that he had brought to them. They would meet with the first victim's parents on Wednesday morning.

The Chief said that he did not envy her. He always dreaded having to talk to parents who had lost a child.

As they drove back, she asked if they wanted to eat out or go home.

Trey smiled and said that it was home for him.

Johnnie nodded and said that he was for something simple with the least amount of effort possible.

Alex agreed and suggested they get to work early the next day and prepare for what she thought would be a stressful day and likely a long one.

She figured that she would order in her favorite Thai dinner and make it an early evening.

8 The Parents

Matt had come home in the wee early morning hours and collapsed into bed. Alex was awake early and quietly got ready for work. She left the coffee on, two hard boiled eggs on the counter and a bowl of oatmeal by the microwave for him and after eating one soft-boiled egg and having coffee she rolled her bike to the elevator.

She and Johnnie rode silently into work. It was clear to her that the nature of the case seemed to suck the energy from a person. She had some dread about the next two days. She knew she would be opening deep wounds with all the parents and knew the impact that would have on them and on her and Trey as well.

The sun was just coming up as they arrived at the station. She thought about Bill and Trevor and wondered how their surveillance had gone. She then realized that she was going to miss not having her half of a bear claw with her coffee because the two of them were the ones that always came in with the box of rolls and donuts.

As she and Johnnie approached her desk, she smiled and wondered how the donut box had arrived at her desk. There was a note on the box that said that it would take two trays of cookies to make up for making him miss his morning donut. It was signed Trevor.

Alex called Trevor and thanked him for being so thoughtful and asked him how the night had been.

She learned that Levi had stayed on the farm for the night and had not yet been spotted. Trevor commented that he and Bill had taken turns flying the drone that they had with them as entertainment and that it was a great refresher.

He commented that they had taken turns sleeping in the back seat.

Alex let him know that she would be out his way to interview the parents of the first victim and she would be glad to bring them lunch.

Trevor said that he hoped that Levi would go back to Cincinnati before then but if they were still parked in the forest across from the farm field, he would let her know.

Alex thanked him for thinking about the donuts and let him know that he had made her day.

He laughed and said that she was easy to satisfy.

After she hung up Johnnie commented that Trevor had really come a long way and was now one of her strongest advocates.

Trey walked in with his cup of coffee and pointed to the half bear claw on his desk. He looked at the message and commented that the long hand of the Trevor was very welcome.

Dr. Rogers walked up to Johnnie and handed him six reports and said that three were associated with the Cincinnati body part operation and three were associated with the Cleveland operation. He added that he had looked at the other missing person reports but most did not have any information that let him do anything more.

He looked in the donut box and asked if he could have a glazed cake donut.

Alex thanked him for bringing up the reports and said that he should take several donuts because two of the team were not going to be coming into the office.

The Chief walked in and came over and helped himself to a jelly filled roll. He looked at Alex and asked her if she was ready for a really tough day.

Alex shook her head and said there was no way to get ready to open the wounds of parents who had lost their daughter, but she would save her crying until she and Trey were back in their car.

The Chief nodded and said that he had visited several parents with the bad news about their child and it had affected him for months. He asked if the team was still holding sessions with the department therapist.

Alex nodded and said that the team considered her an essential part of the work they did.

"Good, see you Friday morning," the Chief said as he headed for his office.

Dr. Rogers said thanks for the donut and left as well.

Alex asked Johnny to stand by during the day and as they finished an interview, she would call him if she had any additional sleuthing requests.

Johnnie said that he was going to go back to the apartment and work from home.

Alex nodded and said that was a good idea. She signaled Trey for them to go and led the way to the car.

Trey confessed that he would rather be in a gun battle then to do the parent interviews. It was really hard for him to watch the pain of their loss resurface. He added that she should not expect any questions from him.

Alex agreed and said that they could cry on each other's shoulders after they left the house.

Sheriff Milster met them when they arrived. He asked whether they wanted him to drive to each place they would be going.

Alex replied that she wanted the meetings with each family to be as low key as possible and she preferred not to use a marked police car.

Sheriff Milster said that would be no problem and that he would drive an unmarked police car that the unit had just acquired. It would be the first time he would have a chance to try it out.

Alex nodded and said that she was all in for him to drive.

Sheriff Milster made a call to the first couple to verify that they were still agreeable to going through their daughter's disappearance.

The drive took them about twenty minutes and when they arrived, they drove up the lane of a house that was in the center of a large yard that was probably an acre in size.

Alex took in the roses along the front of the house and the evenly trimmed low hedge along the side of the garage. She noted the ten-foot diameter round garden in the middle of the front yard with brown eyed Susan flowers giving it a warm appearance. She hoped when she left the flowers would lift her spirit up after the interview.

Sheriff Milster rang the doorbell and was warmly greeted and invited in.

He introduced Alex and Trey as Cincinnati detectives that he had enrolled to see if they could help with the cold cases that he had not been able to solve.

Alex was surprised when the mother commented that she had seen her on the news and had been impressed with the fact that each time the report was about a case that she had solved. The one she recalled the most and thought about often was when she had solved the case of a young girl missing for fifteen years and had saved her and her two daughters. She admitted it had made her cry for several weeks. She asked if Alex still had contact with that young woman.

Alex smiled and said that she did and that she and her two daughters were doing well.

The father commented that he hoped she could pull off another miracle.

Alex replied that she hoped so too but miracles were few and far between. She added that what she would promise was to capture and if justice played out the way she hoped she would see the perpetrator go to the gas chamber.

The mother smiled and said that would at least let them close a door to a painful section of their minds.

Alex nodded and confessed that the questions she was going to ask would be personal and potentially painful. She said that it was one of the more difficult parts of her work.

The mother held up her hand and asked if they could sit around the kitchen table. She offered to serve cookies, hot or cold tea, coffee, or milk.

Alex thanked her and said that the kitchen would be a great place and that a cup of coffee would be great.

The five of them sat down and after the drinks were poured the mother said she was ready for the questions and that Alex should understand that she and her husband were very appreciative of having someone looking once again into the case. They were not expecting a miracle but were hoping for closure.

Alex nodded and asked if either of them remembered anything about the day their daughter went missing that stood out.

There was silence for a few moments then the mother said that the morning had been like all other school mornings. She had called for her daughter to come down for breakfast multiple times. At the last moment, her daughter had rushed down, drank her glass of milk, took a bite of her egg, grabbed two strips of bacon, ran out of the house with her backpack and ran to the end of the lane as the bus arrived.

She wiped a tear from her eyes and said that she had not been given a hug.

Alex took a bite of the cookie and a sip of coffee. She looked at the cookie, said it was delicious and asked what it was called.

The mother smiled and said that it was a short bread cookie with a twist that she had added. She then added that it had been her daughter's favorite.

Alex nodded, she then looked at the father and asked what he remembered about the day his daughter went missing.

He shook his head and said he remembered rushing to the school because he was running late and was supposed to pick her up after her cheer leading practice. When he got there, he could not locate her and asked the other cheer leaders if they knew where she was. They let him know that she had not been at practice. They all thought that she had gone home early.

He then called the house only to learn she was not home. He walked through the entire school asking about her and one grounds keeper said he had seen her walking out with one of the young men, but he had no clue about who it was.

He had then walked the entire school grounds and then driven home having a feeling of dread.

They had called Sheriff Kagle, now retired, to ask him to have his team keep an eye out for her. He said he would do it and that they should come in the following day if she was still missing and put in a missing person report.

That was now at least twelve years ago.

Alex asked if they had the names of their daughter's friends.

The mother got up and returned with a yearbook and said that all of their daughter's friends had a star on the upper right corner and often a note on the edge of the page. She pointed to the tabs that she had put on each page that had a friend marked.

She said that she had talked to each of her daughter's friends at the time of the disappearance but had never gotten anything that was of any help. She had asked about boyfriends but none of her friends thought she had one.

Alex asked if it was possible for her to borrow the yearbook so she could go through it in detail.

The mother nodded and said that she hoped that Alex would have better luck with it than she had, and she added that of course she wanted it returned.

Alex said that she would indeed return it. She asked if there was a hair sample that she might get so they could check for DNA. She also asked for some hair from each of them so that she could use them to make a positive match if necessary.

The father asked if she was asking because she had a body.

Alex shook her head and said that she did not, but she wanted to be prepared with the DNA so that she would not need to ask for it later.

The mother smiled and said that it made her sad to think what the DNA might uncover but she was pleased with the way Alex was preparing. It was more than anyone else had done to date.

She left the room and came back with three brushes and put them in zip lock bags and used a sharpie to put her name, her daughter's name, and her husband's name on them and put them on the table. She tapped her finger on the yearbook and said that she wanted it back and she wanted her daughter's hairbrush back but the other two did not matter.

Alex thanked her for being willing to provide the materials with which she hoped to solve the case.

She asked Sheriff Milster if he had evidence bags and if he could get them to put in what they were gathering.

She then smiled and said there was only one more very important question. She shared the fact that she used cookies, brownies, and muffins to bribe her co-workers and she handed out bags of chocolate to folks like Sheriff Milster in hopes of getting their cooperation. She would love to add the delicious short bread cookie to the cookie list she currently baked.

The mother smiled and said that she would be the first person that she was going to share her recipe with, and she hoped that it would help Alex solve the case.

She got up and walked to the counter, wrote for a few minutes, and returned with a note that had the recipe and the preparation instructions.

She smiled and thanked Alex for the way she had conducted such a personal interview with such a warm touch.

Alex nodded and said that she would see if she could do justice to the cookie recipe. She had a very demanding team who would give her their honest feedback.

The Sheriff returned with the evidence bags. Trey put the two brushes into one evidence bag and the yearbook into the larger evidence bag and then sealed both of them and signed his name.

He asked to have both Alex and the Sheriff sign it as well.

The Sheriff nodded and said that it was a good idea to treat the evidence in the proper fashion.

Alex stood up and gave the mother a hug and wished her the best and that she would personally contact her when she solved the case.

She then shook the father's hand.

He smiled and asked if he was going to get a hug from her.

Alex reached up and pulled him into a hug.

Trey stood up and got a hug from the mother and a handshake and back slap from the father.

Sheriff Kagle shook hands and said that he would stay in close contact with Alex.

He led the way out to his car.

The yellow brown eyed Susan Garden did make her feel better, but she was really sad because she did not expect to find their daughter, Heather, alive.

Once in the car Alex let out a sigh. She said that the interview had gone much better then she had expected, and the attitude of the parents had made it less stressful then she had thought it would be. It was clear to her that they missed their daughter but had managed to move on with their lives.

Sheriff Kagle looked at her and complimented her with how she had won both parents over and had gotten more than anyone else had ever gotten. He said that he had never seen the yearbook and he had been in the department when their daughter went missing.

Alex said that she was sure the killer had his picture in the yearbook, and she had a firsthand witness that would verify it before morning.

She added that she thought that by the weekend she would have the DNA match that would nail the killer.

Sheriff Kagle shook his head and said that he hoped so because it had been a weight around his neck since he was a young cop.

Alex asked if he had a place in mind for lunch.

He said that he liked to go to a small mom and pop diner which featured a variety of burgers with fries, tater tots or onion rings on the side.

They would be early and hopefully ahead of the crowd because he had never seen the place empty. There was always a huge crowd that always seemed to fill the place.

Alex said that it sounded like they would get a good lunch. They should have lunch and get prepared for their next interview.

After a quick lunch Alex said that she did not think the next interview session was going to be as smooth as the first because the parents would have had less time grieving and would still be looking for information and answers about their missing daughter.

Sheriff Kagle agreed that the next three sessions would be tougher because the parents were still processing the grief and they were in the angry stage where they were looking for someone to blame. He said that he and his folks had been the focus of that anger.

Alex nodded and said she understood their anger and that their daughter's disappearance had happened in the last few months. She hoped that they would cooperate, but she understood their frustration and anger.

The Sheriff said that their next victim had been the one that had come home for the weekend, had gone hiking and had not returned. The parents had driven every country road that they thought she might have hiked along and had even gone up and down a small local creek hoping to find her. They had been angry with his desk help who told them that they would need to wait twenty-four hours to put in a missing person's report. He was not sure, but he had a suspicion that they were racist.

Alex looked at Trey and asked him if he would take the lead for this interview.

The Sheriff again went first and made the introductions.

Alex came in last and when the introductions were made, Trey got a handshake from the mother and father, and she got a nod from each of them.

They were led into the living room and asked to sit down.

Alex sat down and listened as Trey asked the questions. It was apparent that the attitude was more hostile, and the sheriff was asked repeatedly whether his unit was continuing the search.

Trey got the samples of hair. He had evidence bags that the sheriff had provided and put the hair into them and handed them to the Sheriff.

He asked for the most recent picture that he might get a copy of and received sharp reply that the Sheriff already had a picture.

Trey looked over at Alex and the Sheriff and asked if they had any other questions.

Alex asked what the last word each of them had shared with their daughter.

The father let out an expletive and asked what that had to do with finding his daughter. The mother admonished her husband and said that her last words had been to wish her daughter a good hike and that she would have her favorite dinner ready when she got back and then she had given her a hug.

Alex nodded and said that is what her mother always promised when she went on a hike, and she always took the hike with that thought in mind. She added that she was sure that was the thought her daughter had with her during her hike.

The mother nodded and asked what role Alex had on the case.

Alex smiled and said that she was the lead detective on the case.

The mother nodded and smiled, and she said that the family reputation must have gotten out. She added that personally she was the normal one in the family, but she kept a low profile.

Alex nodded and replied that she was often taken by surprise that after more than a hundred years color was still such a barrier for people to get along.

The husband stood up and declared the meeting was over and walked out.

The wife stood up and apologized and said that the daughter had been his favorite child and he had withdrawn and had refused to go to counseling with the rest of the family.

Alex nodded and apologized for resurfacing the pain, but she added that she needed to understand firsthand what had happened and might be back to personally hike the roads her daughter might have taken.

The mother nodded and said that if she did come out to make the hike, she wanted to accompany her because she was not sure about the reception she might get if she hiked alone.

Alex thanked her and she said she would let her know.

She then asked the Sheriff to lead the way back to the car.

Once in the car the Sheriff again complimented her and said that he was learning a lot about how to manage grieving parents.

Alex nodded and replied that she followed a simple saying, "treat others the way you wish to be treated." She added that she also imagined or visualized how a person might be feeling in the specific situation they found themselves in.

Sheriff Kagle asked if they should follow the same approach for the interview process the next day.

Alex nodded and said she and Trey would meet him in the morning and he could take them to each interview.

Once back to her car she asked Trey to drive.

She made a call to Matt and asked him to schedule a time early Friday morning to be at the station to look through the yearbook to see if he could make an identification of the person he saw at the concert on the green.

She then called the Chief to update him.

After that she called Trevor to see how surveillance was going.

9 The Farm

*T*he interview with the last two parents was better than the second one had been. They learned that one of the young women had gone to an outdoor show that featured the battle between the local Indians and the settlers of the time that used real horses in a large outdoor venue. One couple came forward and said they thought that they had seen the missing young woman talking to a slender man dressed in black jeans wearing a blue T-shirt, but they had not been close enough to see much more.

The second missing young woman had gone to a concert in downtown Columbus and had never come home. The follow-up investigation did not come up with any leads.

Sheriff Milster said that he wished they had come up with more during the interviews.

Alex told him that she thought they had what they needed to solve the case.

Early Friday morning she had Matt sit down in one of the huddle rooms with Trey and go through the yearbook to see if he could identify the person he had seen in the park. She had covered the names so that he would have to pick the picture based on only facial recognition.

She had the process officially captured by the department film crew who were also told they would likely be witnesses in court if Matt was asked about his identification of the perpetrator.

When Matt turned to the M's he stopped and pointed to a picture and said that it was the person sitting on the lawn at the concert.

Alex thanked him and made sure the film crew closed with a close up shot of the yearbook picture with the name covered and then with the cover removed so the name, Levi Aram Misle was clearly visible.

She thanked everyone and emphasized that the film was to be treated and handled as evidence.

She looked at the time and said it was time to get ready for the search of each of the properties.

She called Bill and asked where he was, and he said they were at a downtown grocery store shopping. He commented that he thought that Levi may have made them. He guessed that following him into the store might not have been wise.

Alex said that Levi could be arrested. She said that his properties would be searched and hopefully the case would be closed.

Bill said he had to go and hung up.

Alex walked into the Chief's office and said that it was time to do the searches and he should have the properties seized.

The Chief nodded and made a call and then led the way to his car.

Alex said that she needed to go to the locker room to get her Kevlar outfit.

Trey said he would do the same.

The Chief picked up his gym bag and said he had his. He would put it on when he got to the farm.

Alex said that Bill had been instructed to make the arrest. She suggested searching the farm first.

She took the seat behind the Chief and Trey took the passenger seat. Johnnie sat behind Trey and put his drone carrier between him and Alex.

The Chief nodded and took the highway north.

Alex's phone buzzed. It was Bill calling to let her know that Levi had escaped.

Alex was silent for a moment and then decided to reassign Bill and Trevor.

Alex suggested that they drive to the farm, and they could assist on the search for bodies. She asked them to bring both of their drones.

Levi had spotted the two that seemed to be following him. He made a bee line to his truck and sped out of the city.

He figured he would go to the farm where he had supplies and then head out of the state. He wondered how he had been made. As he drove, he thought about his situation and figured even the farm might not be safe. He decided to go to the far corner of the property where there was a shed where one of the huge tractors was kept. He could get a good view of the house and much of the surroundings from the roof.

He was glad that he kept his rifle and shotgun under the back seat of the truck. He at least had the firepower to defend himself or to take action if he thought it would help him.

Alex commented that she had Levi dead to rights but now she needed bodies. She looked over to Johnnie and said that when they got to the farm, he should take the lead and with Bill and Trevor search the place for grave sites.

Johnnie nodded and said that the Canadian border case had given all of them practice in identifying the very slight depressions on a forest floor that an aged grave made. He would organize the search on each side of the road leading to the little lake where they had spotted Levi fishing. It seemed to be a natural place to bury bodies.

Alex nodded and said that she and Trey would search the outbuildings. She asked the Chief to take the farmhouse with a set of officers.

The Chief smiled and said that it felt good being in on the action and having someone else take the lead.

Alex asked if he wanted the lead.

He replied that he liked it just the way it was coming down.

He was stopped at the end of the driveway to the farm by one of the Sheriff's deputies. The deputy recognized Alex and said that Sheriff Milster was at the house waiting for them.

Alex thanked him for the information.

Alex let him know that she had two of her team coming in behind her.

The Chief parked next to the Sheriff's car.

After a brief handshake Alex said that they should check the place out.

The Chief and the Sheriff headed for the house with four other officers.

Alex asked two officers to accompany her, and she headed for the largest of what she thought of as barns.

It was apparent that the larger barn was set up to be a milking barn and it seemed to still be a functioning one. She walked around until she was sure there was nothing to find.

She asked one of the deputies to call out to the two at the end of the driveway and to hold anyone coming to the farm to do the milking because she did not want anyone in until the search was over.

She then led the way to the second barn and decided it was the storage barn. It held stacks of bags and was filled with hay and bales of straw. An orange forklift was parked with its prongs inserted into a pallet stacked with ground feed for the cows.

She saw the ladder going up and asked one of the deputies to take a look. He called back that it just held old rusty equipment.

Alex did a thorough check. She did not expect to find anything useful and said that the search was over, and they should go outside.

Johnnie walked out to the end of the road leading back to the lake and found a tree that had fallen over. It was in the shade and provided a good place to sit. He took Gunjfor out of her carrying case and took her for an initial warmup spin. He decided that he would search on one side of the road. He would have Trevor search the other side and Bill could search around the lake.

He had just finished mounting Gunjifor's weapon when Bill and Trevor arrived.

Trevor saw the gun in Gunjfor's gun holder. He asked which grave Johnnie planned to shoot.

Johnnie smiled as replied he was just going to be ready to get even with anyone who ticked him off.

He put a quick call in to Alex to let her know that the body search team was soon to be searching the grounds.

Levi drove slowly around to where the road was running along the back corner of his farm. He took out his deer hunting rifle, mounted the scope and made sure he had some extra ammunition with him. He then climbed up on the roof and slowly scanned the house and the two barns. He watched as four people came out of the main barn.

He immediately recognized the Black woman. She had been his first choice when he had been searching for his next victim. Now he realized she was some kind of law. He now recalled seeing her in the news. He shook his head at the bad luck he had stepped into.

He decided to kill her. He moved into a better position, carefully adjusted his rifle, took notice of the wind, and figured the drop for the distance. She would be just like any deer that he shot. It would be one to the heart and then he would hightail it out of the country.

He needed to withdraw as much money as he could from his local bank. He also had a huge sum of money he would need to get transferred to a new account.

Then his mind refocused on the smaller barn. The door had been left partially open and one of the deputies walked out in the lead. Then a tall plain clothed policeman and then the petite Black policeman. She was walking out in perfect position when he slowly squeezed the trigger.

He watched her fly back into the deputy behind her and lay on the ground at his feet. He picked up his ejected casing and quickly made his way down from the shed roof and ran to his truck. He threw everything to the floor behind the driver's seat and jumped in behind the wheel and roared out to the highway. He knew he needed to get away as quickly as possible.

Alex walked out and was about to head for the house when she felt that someone had kicked her hard in the center of her chest. She flew backwards into the person behind her. She stayed down as she tried to get her breath back. It was clear to her that she had been hit hard and had suffered some sort of significant injury. She closed her eyes and focused on getting her breath back.

Trey and the two police officers had their guns drawn and were trying to located the shooter.

Johnnie heard the shot. He immediately took Gunjfor as far above the tree line as he could and spotted the black truck barreling along the road out beyond the other side of the lake.

He flew Gunjfor as fast as he could toward the intersection where the smaller road joined the main state highway. He dove Gunjfor towards the truck at the fastest speed possible and fired a series of shots at the truck. He was sure he had hit it at least five times but it did not stop the truck.

He had to land Gunjfor because her battery was done and there was no more power left to get her back.

He got up and raced over to where Alex was now sitting up against the barn. He could hear that emergency vehicle as it came down the lane.

Alex closed her eyes as she tried to recover her breath.

The Chief and the Sheriff and all the rest were standing around her as the EMT group pushed passed them.

They stopped when they saw Alex sitting by the barn. The lead asked where she had been hit.

Alex put her finger through her suit jacket and then pointed to where the flattened bullet had bonded with her Kevlar vest.

The EMT asked everyone to get back so they could back their unit in as close as possible. He then asked Alex if she could stand and be helped into the unit. He said that the team had one female member who he introduced and then asked her to examine Alex. Once Alex had been helped in, he closed the back doors.

Alex sat down on the side bench and leaned against the side of the unit. She was amazed by the impact that the bullet had delivered.

She was still trying to catch her breath.

The female EMT opened her blouse and commented that Alex was lucky to be alive because the bullet had hit almost directly over her heart. Her heart was probably working hard to recover from being shocked. She would probably need to spend a couple of days in the hospital under observation.

Alex shook her head and said that wasn't going to happen at the moment. She was going to rest for a moment and then she was going to Cincinnati to search through a house where she hoped to get the evidence that would put the person who had shot her in prison.

She buttoned up her blouse and said she would like to get out.

The EMT shook her head and opened the doors.

Alex took Trey's hand as he helped her down. She smiled and asked why he was standing in front of everyone else.

He looked at her and said that he knew she would be wanting to get out and get to Cincinnati.

Alex nodded and asked if anyone had figured out where the shot had come from.

Johnnie said that he had when he took Gunjfor up after the shot. There was a shed at the corner of the property that was the most likely location. He explained that he had gotten five shots at the black truck, but it had gotten away.

He explained that Gunjfor's battery had run low, and he had landed her in the forest at the corner of the property.

Alex complimented him on his quick reaction and asked him to continue the body search after he had Gunjfor back in action.

She looked over to where Bill and Trevor were standing and asked if they had found any possible grave sites.

Bill shook his head in the negative, but Trevor gave a thumbs up. He said he had about a half a dozen potential graves.

Johnnie then added that he had a similar number in the area where he had been searching.

Alex looked at the Chief and asked if Cincinnati could provide additional personnel that could work with Sheriff Milster and his folks and begin to dig up the potential graves.

Sheriff Milster shook his head and said that it was hard to believe they had more than twelve potential grave sites and her team had only looked for less than an hour.

He asked one of the deputies to drive Johnnie out to get his drone.

He then looked at Alex and asked how deep he thought the graves would be.

Alex replied she had no clue and that he should dig one up to determine the depth. She then asked why he wanted to know.

He replied that he wanted to use a backhoe to dig about two thirds of the way down and then proceed by hand shovel until the remains were found then the forensics team could do the rest. That would speed up the recovery and reduce the amount of work and the number of people he would need.

Alex thought that was a good idea. She added that she wanted to keep this out of the news until she at least captured the killer so he would need to use people that he trusted to keep quiet.

Levi knew that he had to get off the road as soon as he could. He remembered an old, abandoned barn not far from the main interstate and close to a couple of used car lots. Because of the three bullet stars on the back window, he knew he had to abandon his truck and get out of the area as soon as possible.

He had five hundred dollars in cash and hoped that the car lot had a car that still ran but would not cost more than that.

He organized everything he planned to take with him and put it in the back of the truck. Then he walked out to the first used car lot.

He spotted two cars that were marked up as fix up deals.

He asked the lot dealer about them and was told that if he paid four hundred in cash, he could drive out with the title in hand but there would be no refunds. The cars would run but they were at the end of life.

Levi asked to listen to both cars running. He could hear a knock in one. The other seemed to run smoothly so he chose it.

The dealer gave him the deed for the car and said the he hoped it was what he wanted.

Levi adjusted the mirrors, put the seat where it seemed about right. The gas gauge was nearly empty. There were several gas stations within sight.

He felt like he was sitting in a bathtub looking over its edge as he drove.

He drove slowly out and in the opposite direction of where his truck was parked. After a few miles he turned back and stopped at a gas station, filled the car up, checked the oil level which he had to top off. He figured that using oil was probably an issue, so he bought two quarts and put them in the trunk.

He then drove back to the barn and put all of the stuff he had in the trunk and drove back to the highway and headed west.

Alex sat in the passenger seat and leaned back and relaxed.

She knew that she had once again been lucky. She took the time to call Matt and let him know that she had been shot but was doing fine.

Matt asked if she had gotten the shooter.

Alex replied that she had not even seen the shooter, but that Johnnie had gotten a few shots at the shooter and that the shooter was very likely the guy he had identified.

Matt asked what she was up to for the rest of the day.

She replied that she was on the way to the house to search for any evidence that it might hold.

He wished her luck and said he would check on her after she was done at the house.

10 The House

lex relaxed and lay back in her seat. She closed her eyes and thought through the upcoming search. She was still wearing her bulletproof vest but was not expecting any more gunfire.

She wondered where Levi would go and how he might be trying to escape. She figured he would try to change vehicles.

She called Johnnie and asked if he had researched Levi's finances.

Johnnie replied that things had moved so fast that he had not had time to do so. He said that as soon as he got to where he could get a Wi-Fi connection he would do so.

Alex told him to finish the body search and then go after the finances.

She looked over to the Chief and commented that Johnnie was one of the team's star members. He was superfast at hacking, had been the only one who had spotted and shot at the shooter and was now leading the effort to recover bodies.

The Chief nodded and said that he had no knowledge of any hacking being done in his organization, but he agreed with everything else.

He maneuvered up the winding Mt Hill road and then turned up a side street and parked behind one of the squad cars.

The senior officer greeted him. He told him that it was time to searched the house.

Eight patrolmen walked up the long walk to the front door. The officer in charge said he had two more officers in back in case anyone tried to leave. Those going in the front were assigned two to a floor.

He led the way up.

When Alex had to stop to catch her breath, she knew that she had most likely been hurt more seriously than she had expected.

She looked over at Trey and told him that as soon as they had any evidence she was going to the hospital.

Trey put her arm over his shoulder and literally picked her up and walked the rest of the way up carrying her.

As they got inside, they heard a shout from the top floor that they needed to come up immediately.

Trey looked around and found a small elevator. He got in and pulled Alex to him and pressed the button for the third floor. When the door opened they were in a room that made both of the stop in shock. The room they were in was full of mounted skulls.

Alex stopped. She heard the Chief loudly curse and say that he had never expected to find such a horror chamber.

The two patrolmen who had come up first were still holding their weapons at the ready.

Alex suggested that they put them away and that the room was off limits to everyone. She led Trey out of the room. Once she was out, she made a call to Dr. Rogers and told him that he needed to bring his team to examine and process more skulls than she could count. She said that she was keeping everyone away until he was at the scene, then she would take a tour with him before leaving.

She found a chair and sat down and took some deep breaths.

A short time later, she was surprised when Matt and his team followed Dr. Rogers and his team up the stairs.

She looked over at Trey who nodded his head in the affirmative.

She stood up and followed Dr. Rogers into the room.

Dr. Rogers asked his team to stay behind, and he led the way in. He kept mumbling, "Oh my god," as he walked through the four rooms.

He pointed to the pictures and the descriptions that each skull had at the base of the stand holding the skull.

When they got to the very back room, the stand in front of the fireplace had a large star on it. When they looked at the picture and the note, Alex knew they had found the young lady that had been taken from her high school. She was the first victim.

She looked at the Dr. and said that she had hair samples of the young lady as well as from her parents. She would have all her evidence delivered to him at the morgue. She said that how he handled the skulls for processing was up to him.

On the way-out Alex pointed to a door at the side of the room. The room led into the turret of the house. It had windows around two thirds of it. The door was on the back side of the turret. The room had a great view of downtown Cincinnati.

Alex walked up to the far side near the windows to a couch. She looked at the cushions and figured that this was a couch where Levi often sat.

The room was set up like a surgical arena with a stainless-steel table at its center and counters all around it.

It was clear to both of them that it was the skull preparation room.

Dr. Rogers said that he would set up his analysis room at the table and first process each skull locally and have samples taken to the morgue for more detail analysis.

Alex said that she had to leave and go to the hospital because she had been shot and was feeling the effects long after she had expected to.

He said that he wondered what Matt and his team were doing following him up all the stairs.

When she got back to the entrance to what she now thought of as "the Skull Museum," Matt pointed to a body board and asked her to lie down.

She nodded and let him help her to do that.

The rest of the EMT team went into action and strapped her to the board and then slowly carried her down three flights of stairs inside of the house and three flights of stairs leading to the street.

Once they were in the EMT unit, they took her vitals and began a conversation with the hospital emergency staff.

Alex decided that closing her eyes and relaxing was the only way to handle the situation.

The attending emergency room Dr. told her he was going to give her a mild sedative to let her body relax and that she would be put into an intensive care unit as soon as it was ready and that she would be staying at least overnight.

She asked if it was really necessary.

Matt said that he had gotten a detailed description of what had happened from Trey and was sure that it was necessary.

He had just finished when Trey walked in.

Matt looked at Trey and thanked him for the call. He said that he and his team needed to get back on duty because it was the beginning of the rush hour when bad things would be happening.

Trey nodded and said he would stay until Alex was in the intensive care unit.

Alex was just about to ask Trey why he had called Matt when the nurse came in with a person pushing a unit that turned out to be an x ray machine.

The technician asked everyone to get out of the room and he then pushed a plate behind Alex's back and took a series of pictures. He then took the plated and put it on the cart and wheeled the unit out.

Trey came back in and said he had called Matt while she was sitting trying to recover and he didn't want to hear any complaints. She should just think about the time she had almost killed him by hiding him in an ice water puddle.

Alex smiled, nodded, and said that she was glad he had her back.

A few moments later another doctor came in and said that he had just looked at her x rays and said she had a partially collapse lung and that once she was in intensive care they were going to put her on an oxygen assist that would provide extra pressure to the lung as she breathed in to see if after an overnight stay the lung would go back to normal.

He added that she would most likely be in the hospital over the weekend.

Alex let out a groan and said that being in the hospital was not what she had planned for the weekend. She knew that Matt would have the weekend off because they had arranged for a ride along the Loveland trail for his team. They had invited Johnnie to join them.

She called Johnnie and asked him how the finding of graves was going.

Johnnie said that they had found thirty-two graves so far but only one had been dug up.

Bill had found bodies on the far side of the lake back up into the woods which had not been counted or marked. He had only started finding them when the sun was into the late afternoon. Before then he could not see the grave depressions.

He asked her how she was feeling.

Alex replied that she was in the hospital and would soon be in intensive care for the weekend.

There was silence on the phone for a long period.

Alex was about to ask if he was still on the line when he spoke up.

He said that he, Bill, and Trevor would be in to visit and did she want any Thai food for dinner.

Alex smiled and said that she did and anything they got would be good.

Johnnie added that he was about to call her to let her know that he would not be able to go on the bike ride because he, Bill and Trevor had agreed that they needed to be on hand when the digging started in earnest. He had called Dr. Rogers to let him know about the bodies that would need processing and that his team needed to be on site.

Alex was interrupted when the nursing team that was going to move her to the intensive care unit entered.

Alex asked her if visitors would be allowed that evening. When she got a no, she told Johnnie to postpone any visit until the following day.

Johnnie said he understood and wished her a good night.

Alex hung up and lay back and took a deep breath. She felt exhausted.

The nurse came in and said that there were two people outside of the room that she thought were police officers. One was requesting her clothes to take in as evidence and the other told her to say that Sandra had her back.

Alex realized that the Chief had assigned a protection detail for her. She thanked the nurse for the information and said that her clothes should be given to the person seeking it as evidence and to let the other officer know that she appreciated being protected by such a wonderful person.

The nurse suddenly turned and seemed to be trying to shield Alex.

She heard the Chief identify himself.

Alex let the nurse know that it was safe.

The Chief came to the end of the bed and asked how she was doing.

Alex asked what was up and why the protection detail?

The Chief replied that the press had found out about the raid at the house at Mount Healthy and then had found out about the farm.

The officer at the farm had called and let him know that they had shot down a camera drone that belonged to a local independent reporter.

It was almost immediate that the raids made the news and that a Black policewoman had been seen being taken away in an emergency vehicle.

There are other Black police officers, but you are the one that made the news.

The Chief came over to the head of the bed and whispered that it was under her pillow.

Alex knew immediately that he had put a weapon under her pillow.

She thanked him for putting a guard outside her door and said he should make sure her guards used their armor.

The Chief nodded and wished her a good night and that he would be back in the morning.

Alex wondered if she would be able to fall asleep but after making sure her weapon would not be discovered she was almost immediately asleep.

The room was dark when she heard gunfire. She rolled out of the bed and crouched on the floor. The door opened, a rapid volley of bullets hit the bed, and she had to roll to get away from the barrage.

She jumped up and ran to the door and slid out along the floor. That slide almost made her faint. She looked down the hallway but could not find the shooter.

She crawled over to where a police officer was sitting against the wall. It was the officer that had stood guard for Trey when he was in the hospital. She checked his vitals and was relieved to get a pulse. She then went to where the nurse was lying and applied pressure to the shoulder wound that was bleeding.

A hand pulled her away as she was told by a feminine voice that she should get back in bed because her butt was showing.

Alex stood up and almost wanted to laugh but as she looked around, she realized that not only was the shooter a serial killer he was an angry cornered animal seeking revenge and would go after anyone that he felt was a threat.

She watched as a blue wave seemed to roll down the hallway toward her.

She looked at the police officer sitting against the wall, and he gave her a thumbs up. He pulled open his shirt to show her his Kevlar vest.

She smiled and thanked him for guarding her and for buying the vest.

She went back into the ICU and sat down after putting her weapon in the closet under some pillows. She looked at the bed where one of the pillows was full of holes. It had fallen forward when she jumped out and she was sure that in the dark it looked like a body.

About a half an hour later two hospital personnel came in to wheel out the bullet riddled bed. Alex stopped them and asked if there was anyone in the hallway to accept the bed as evidence.

One of them returned and said that the officer in charge had said that he would see that it was handled as evidence.

They then wheeled in a new bed.

Alex retrieved her weapon, turned the bed so she faced the door and then climbed into it. A male nurse came in and hooked her up to the monitoring equipment and the oxygen.

She was asleep almost instantly.

It was five thirty in the morning when a new female nurse came in, introduced herself and took her vitals.

Alex next woke up at eight when the attending physician came in to see how she was doing.

The Chief came in a short time later to let her know that the officer that had been shot was recovering well and said that she should know that many of his buddies had teased him about him buying his own Kevlar suit, but he had just told him that he was eternally grateful that he had.

Alex asked how the Chief's request for the force to buy vests for every officer was going.

He shook his head and said that the budget constraints were keeping it from getting any traction.

Alex asked if she arranged a donation of body armor would he see that every officer received them.

The Chief nodded and said that would be easy.

Alex said that he should set up a group to manage such a donation and she would make sure they got the suits.

She then asked how the digging at the farm was going.

The Chief said that they had dug down to the point where they could confirm it was a grave with a body for ten of the graves. Once they got to that point they stopped, and they covered the graves with plywood. Dr. Rogers had called in FBI resources to help with the forensics work but they would only arrive and get started in the coming week. Dr. Rogers had retrieved enough DNA from the about twelve of the skulls and had matched them with data he had but he said that he would need to get DNA samples from the parents for most of the skulls.

Alex thanked him for the update and said he should go home and spent time with Mary-Anne.

She planned to relax and later go for a walk around the hospital hallway with Matt.

Matt walked in about the time that she finished talking.

The Chief said good morning to him and then said she was all his.

Alex gave Matt a kiss and asked what he had in the bag. He opened it and took out a box that had a bear claw and some butter and maple syrup for a pancake.

He said it seemed light but figured it would tide her over to when Johnnie, Bill and Trevor would deliver the Thai lunch they had promised.

She thanked him and said that she needed to rest for a while, but she then wanted to take a walk with him to visit the two that had been shot.

11 Bank Account

*L*evi was shocked when he watched the news about the raid on his house. He was really surprised when the person being put into the ambulance was the detective he had shot. He had no clue how she had survived. When he shot her, he had watched as she flew backwards into the deputy behind her. He knew exactly who it was when he saw the camera zoom in and he recognized the tall Black EMT. They had both been in the park where he had zeroed in on her and one other potential skull.

He shook his head and wondered how he could have been so unlucky to be where one of the most successful detectives happened to be.

He knew that he had hit her, but she must have been wearing some sort of very good bulletproof vest. Even then he was amazed that she had survived. He was sure that he had hit her exactly over her heart and the impact alone should have been enough to kill her.

He had gone to the bank and withdrawn nine thousand dollars and had transferred most of the rest to a different bank so he would have access to money.

He figured that his investments would most likely be discovered so he went online and split his account over three other financial institutions and each time put a different name on the account. He smiled as he used several of the names from his skull collection. He felt good about honoring his first by using her name on the account where he put the majority of the money.

He was staying in a motel and was angry about having to lower his standard to being cooped up in such a small place. He was especially upset to have had to abandon his pickup. He wondered how anyone could have had a weapon and been able to hit his pickup from so far away. The pickup was a favorite of his that he had purchased when he had started taking care of his parents. It had all the comfort features and a great sound system.

He thought about his nemesis and decided that before leaving the area he was going to shoot her at close range and make sure she got what she deserved. His only regret was that he would not be able to process her skull and mount it in his collection. Thinking about that made him even more angry than he was already. He did not know how he could ever replace such a fine collection.

He loaded his .44 magnum and put a refill in his sweatshirt pocket. He figured he would only have time to empty his gun and then hightail it out of the hospital. He planned to fill her with lead and then hightail it. He would reload when he got back to his car so he would be ready in case he was stopped.

He smiled at the thought of her bullet riddled body bleeding out in her hospital bed. He almost laughed when he thought about her going to the hospital only to be killed in her bed.

He drove to the hospital and parked near an exit of the parking garage. He took note of the cameras but figured that at this point it didn't matter.

He walked in and asked what room his friend was in. He learned the intensive care room that she was in and was informed that there was no visitation allowed. He shook his head as if he were disappointed and left by the door he had entered. He walked slowly around to another entrance and made his way to the wing where the room that she was in. The stairs came out about two rooms away from her room.

He spotted a policeman sitting outside of the door. He didn't say a word but shot him in the chest and watched as he was thrown against the wall and slid to the floor.

A nurse rushed toward him. He was impressed by her courage and shot her in the shoulder instead of the chest. He figured she would live but she would most likely think twice next time about rushing a person with a gun.

He opened the door to the room and stood in with one foot holding the door open. It was dark inside, but he could make out the body in the bed. He emptied his gun and then turned, hurried back to the stairs, and ran down. He then walked calmly out of the hospital. He watched as several squad cars rushed in and the police ran into the hospital.

He then walked to his car and drove slowly back to his hotel room.

He figured it was time to head west to someplace where he could start a new life.

Trey was the first to arrive and come into the intensive care unit. He said he was glad that she had avoided being shot and asked if she had gotten a chance to shoot Levi.

Alex shook her head and said that she had just barely avoided being shot.

A few moments later the Chief walked in and said that she was ruining his weekend.

Alex smiled and said that she was the victim and that he should go easy on her.

He asked if she had fired her weapon.

Alex shook her head in the negative.

The Chief nodded and then said he was doubling the guard at the door, but he figured that Levi would not be back.

Alex agreed and said they would need to find out what kind of car he was driving. She figured he had ditched his truck.

The Chief agreed and said that he would see if Bill and Trevor could check out the used car lots up around the farm.

Alex said that she expected them around lunch time, and she would work with them on that.

The Chief nodded and said that he was going to go to the driving range and try to work out his concern about the situation. He wanted to arrest Levi and lock him up.

Alex agreed and added that she wanted to get him to the gas chamber.

The Chief chuckled and said that it was too bad that for a special case like his there wasn't a torture chamber they could send him to.

Alex smiled and said she agreed.

Matt walked in with a bag and declared that breakfast had arrived. He asked why there were so many police cars and officers around the Hospital.

Alex replied that she was such an attraction that they had all come out to get her autograph.

Matt looked at Trey and asked him the same question and listened as Trey explained.

Matt came over, gave her a hug and kiss, and handed her the breakfast biscuit with sausage and cheese. He said that he had gone light because he knew that Johnnie was bringing in a full Thai offering for lunch.

Alex thanked him and asked him to bring her some of the bags of candy so that when they went for a walk around the hospital, she could give them out.

Matt nodded and said that he would go back to the apartment and bring them back. He asked how many of the bags he should bring.

Alex told him to bring them all.

A police officer came in and excused himself but said that he had to get information for the incident report.

The Chief nodded and said that he was just leaving.

Trey said he was on the way out as well.

Matt said that he was going to go as well and would return for lunch.

The officer looked at Alex and apologized for running her visitors out.

Alex let him know that once she had answered her questions, she was going to take nap.

The officer went through the standard series of questions and within fifteen minutes was done.

She thanked Alex for the information and wished her a speedy recovery.

Alex had no plans on napping. As she ate her sandwich and sipped on her milk, she thought through what she wanted Johnnie, Bill, and Trevor to do. If they had to go back to the farm, she wanted the truck found. She figured it would be close by. When they found the truck, they should look for used car lots where Levi might have purchased a car.

She wanted Johnnie to go after any money that Levi might have. Once it was located, she wanted to strip him of it in a way that would appear to be so legal that no one would challenge it. She wanted him broke. From previous cases, she knew how effective it was to strip someone of their money.

She wondered how much money Levi had. It seemed that he did not work but owned a huge house and a large farm. She figured it had to be in the millions.

She shook her head as she thought about a multimillionaire serial killer that collected the skulls of his victims.

Matt arrived with the bags of candy and Alex got out of bed and pushed her oxygen bottle ahead of her toward the door.

The nurse stopped her and said that she was in intensive care and could not go walking around the hospital.

Alex smiled and replied that she didn't want to arrest her own nurse but would if she obstructed an officer going about her police duty, she would have to make an arrest.

The nurse smiled and said that she had been warned about her and asked that she at least use a walker and let her partner handle the oxygen tank.

Alex handed her a bag of candy and agreed to use the walker.

She then asked for the room numbers of the officer and the nurse that had been shot.

The nurse looked up the room numbers and gave them to her.

The nurse watched as the two police officers guarding the door followed her patient. She looked at the bag and realized it was top quality chocolate and one of her favorites. She knew the ones in the gold covering had a caramel filler.

Alex stopped and handed the two officers a bag each and thanked them for keeping her safe. She had the pistol that the Chief had given out of site in in her gown pocket.

She then went to the room where the police officer, Jack was in.

She knocked at the door and then went in.

She called him by name and thanked him for having been on duty. She handed him a bag of candy and said that the last time she had given him a bag was when he was guarding her partner at the VA hospital.

Jack smiled and said that he would eat all the chocolate by the end of the day. He had been told that he would be released by the end of the day. He planned to go home and stand under a hot shower for hours. He said he would be praying and thanking his maker and her for having inspired him to have purchased the Kevlar outfit.

Alex nodded and said that she knew exactly how a hot steaming shower felt and that she was going to do the same as soon as she could.

Jack then said that he had been ragged because he had purchased his own Kevlar outfit for a substantial part of his monthly income but now, he figured it had been a lifesaving investment.

Alex agreed and said that her vest was currently bagged as evidence and figured his was as well. She asked him his size and told him it would be delivered in the next few days.

He asked what he would owe her for that.

Alex smiled and said that his continued support was all that it would cost.

She told him to enjoy his shower and that it was time for her to see the nurse who had also been shot.

He asked her if she was going after the person who had shot him.

Alex said that she would and that she planned to make sure he would spend the rest of his life in prison.

A few moments later the nurse that had been shot was as surprised as Jack by her visit. She broke down and cried when Alex handed her a bag of candy.

Alex said that she understood the emotion of being shot and realizing how close it was to being killed.

The nurse said that her husband normally worked on Saturdays at Kings Auto Mall but had taken the day off and was bringing in their nine-year-old son and seven-year-old daughter.

Alex handed her two more bags of chocolates and told her it was for the kids.

The nurse smiled and said that she had been told how tough "That Cincinnati's Black Annie Oakley" was but now she would have to add "with a heart of gold," to the moniker.

Alex smiled and thanked her for the compliment and wished her a speedy recovery.

She told Matt that she was ready to get back to her bed.

Shortly after she was back, the intensive care doctor came in and said that she was ahead of him. He had been planning to encourage her to walk the hallways but had heard from the nurse that she was already doing that. He asked her how she felt.

Alex admitted that the walk had tired her out. She shared that she ran three miles at least four times a week and was not used to getting tired so quickly.

The doctor nodded and said that her routine and the strength of her heart was probably what had saved her life. He figured it had put her in intensive care versus the morgue.

Alex smiled and said that statement provided a lot of motivation to get back to her routine.

The doctor nodded and said that she should work back up to it slowly. He suggested that she take two months to work back up to her old routine. He smiled and asked if she sported a six pack.

Alex handed him a bag of candy and said that she would like to show him her six pack, but she was too modest to do so in her current outfit.

The doctor thanked her for the chocolates and said he was going to order an x-ray for later the next day.

Monday morning, he would determine if she was ready for release.

Alex nodded and said that any more time in bed would drive her crazy.

After the doctor left, Matt shared the fact that his EMT team had volunteered to be on duty and had suggested they reschedule their bike ride until she was ready to lead the way.

He planned to be with the team for the evening shift but would come by the following day and then again go on duty for Sunday night.

Alex said that was great because she really was looking forward to the ride with his team.

Lunch was close at hand, and it was not long before Johnnie led the way into the room with Bill and Trevor close behind. Each of them carried a bag of food.

Alex greeted them and thanked them for saving her from the hospital food. She was not going to tell them about the one pot roast meal that she had enjoyed.

Trevor complained how much the price had gone up.

Alex told him to submit an expense report because she was going to talk business over lunch.

After lunch had been dished out, she asked Johnnie to determine where Levi kept his money and to cut him off.

She asked if they would be out at the farm over the weekend.

Bill verified that he was working with the FBI who were sending a dozen people to the site, and he was going to work with them to orient their efforts for the coming week.

Alex asked him to take some time to locate the pickup that she was sure had been abandoned and to see if they could determine what Levi was now driving.

Johnnie excused himself and said he was going to run out to the car and get his computer.

Trevor shouted after him that he should save himself from all the stress and whiz out on a wheelchair.

Alex wondered what had triggered Johnnie.

Bill commented that it seemed that Johnnie was feeling bad about having Levi get away and then the fact that she had been shot at in the hospital had probably been the last straw.

Alex gave a little laugh and commented that Johnnie was the only one on the team who had struck a blow against Levi.

Johnnie returned carrying his computer. He sat down and put his computer on the stool used by the doctor and soon he was smiling. He said he had picked up the trail to Levi's money that he had been moving to a new account. He laughed, then said he had him.

He said that Levi opened up an account for his niece Heather Preston who was seventeen years of age. Levi was listed as the controlling agent.

Alex smiled and asked Johnnie to disappear Levi from the record and put Heather's name in and make everything a part of a trust set up for her and make her parents the ones that the trust would go to incase of her death.

Johnnie hummed away and then he loudly declared, "Done."

Alex then asked if he could transfer the deed for the farm and put it in the trust and do the same for the house.

She asked if Levi had any other assets.

Johnnie was humming away as he kept saying, got it, got it, got it. He said that he had transferred everything into the trust fund under Heather's name. He said that Levi was now penniless, and the trust fund was worth close to ten million dollars.

Alex smiled and said that she figured that she would work with Heather's parents to rename the account The Heather Helping Hands fund and set it up so each parent of one of the victims would get twelve thousand a year for the rest of their lives and when they died and there were no more parents alive the fund would give the money to Charities that each parent had designated into perpetuity in their daughter's name.

Trevor shook his head and commented that it was getting harder and harder for him to come up with a dig at her.

Alex smiled and said that it would not take a very long time for him to recover since she was not going to let up on him.

She suggested that he go home and play with his small kids and spend a few hours with his wife.

Bob smiled and said that it was reassuring to see her getting back into form.

She nodded and said the doctor had asked her to work slowly up to her old self over the next two months and then to get back to her old exercise level. She would do the same with the give and takes.

She asked Johnnie what he was planning to do for the rest of the weekend.

Johnnie smiled and said that he was going to fly Gunjfor and work with Bill and Trevor to find the truck.

12 Escape

*L*evi was in a funk. He thought through what he needed to do. He figured he needed more than the two quarts of oil he had bought so he stopped at an Auto parts store and bought a case of oil and some bottles of thick goo that claimed to reduce the oil a car burned. He was not sure about the claim, but he figured he might as well try it.

He poured one bottle into the oil fill point as instructed.

There was a cash machine in the parking lot, so he decided to withdraw some additional money. He was surprised to be rejected because of insufficient funds. He had put more than ten thousand dollars into that account. He tried with another card that had the same amount in the bank and was rejected again. He looked at the ATM and wondered if it was damaged or not connected to the same system as his cards. The hair on the back of his neck stood on end.

He stopped at a convenience store where his credit cards were again rejected. He paid in cash as he realized that his money was not available to him. He had just shy of ten thousand dollars with him. His entire world was imploding.

He sat in his car for some time thinking about his situation.

He was glad that he had shot that Black detective in her hospital bed. She and her team had ruined his life. He only wished he would have had time to take her head.

He realized that if he managed to get away, he would need to work for a living. The easy life was over.

He thought about going back and getting his truck. He knew that the police were on his property, but they had no idea where he had put the truck. He figured it would take them a long time to discover where he had parked it. It was where no one would go for a long time.

He changed his mind about his truck and headed towards Indiana. He figured he might stop by a distant cousin's place and then go on toward somewhere in the west.

He thought about the time in Idaho when his parents had gone to the Idaho panhandle to visit friends. They had camped at a place near Coeur d'Alene. He had no intention of trying to find the friends, but he remembered thinking that it was a place he would like to live. He figured since he had nowhere else in mind it was a good place to go.

It was early afternoon as he went past where the distant cousin lived. He really didn't know them, nor did he want to get involved with family, so he decided to keeping going at the thunderous speed of fifty-five miles per hour until the sun went down.

He was well into Iowa when he stopped at a motel that had a flashing sign that promised a clean room for sixty-nine dollars. He laughed when he remembered that on his last fishing trip stayed in the Grand Suite of a top-of-the-line hotel. He almost wanted to cry as he was checked by an old guy whose name tag boasted "a clean room at a great price." If the bedroom was ten by ten, he would have been surprised and the sink faucet in the small sink was slowly dripping and there was a rust stripe down to the drain.

He spent part of the evening figuring out which back highways. He wanted to stay off the interstate because he felt they might be looking for him.

Then tuned in to the news to see if there was anything about him being aired on the evening news. He was relieved that there was nothing.

When the best he could then tune in was a show highlighting the capabilities of one of the top tractors on the market he decided to get some sleep

He figured he would be able to make his way west with no problems. He was glad because he had figured out, he was limited to about fifty miles per hour otherwise he generated a large plume of grey smoke.

Johnnie, Bill, and Trevor drove up to the farm early on Sunday. They talked about working together to do one more sweep of the forest to verify that they had found all the graves, and they were going to make sure each grave was clearly marked.

They shared the fact that they had been shocked by how many graves there were. They wondered how Levi had kept his activities hidden from his parents. They figured the parents never walked the woods and when they went to the lake, they probably walked down the road.

There were four officers at the farm. Two were at the entrance lane and two were outside of the house and barn. The two at the house said that all of them would be replaced by four additional officers late in the afternoon and then would be back on duty on Monday morning. One of the officers added that they had been offered help by the FBI and were looking forward to getting back to their normal work hours.

The three walked along the small road to the dock. Johnnie commented that he didn't believe in ghosts but if they existed this would be the place they would haunt.

They sat down and Johnnie put Gunjfor into the air and went slowly through each section of forest verifying the grave sites and searching for any additional ones. Johnnie flew his drone slowly as close to the forest floor as possible and looked for depressions.

They had agreed to use only one drone and since he was the best pilot, he should use Gunjfor.

All three of them were monitoring the video screen.

Johnnie let out a groan as on the far side of the lake, they found one more spot that appeared to be depressed.

Johnnie made another pass and they all agreed that it looked like another grave. Johnnie landed Gunjfor on the suspected grave site and the three walked around the lake to where she was resting. They examined the site and agreed that it was a forty-second grave.

Bill said that since it was in his search area, he would come back with one of the orange stakes to mark it.

Johnnie said that would allow him time to put Gunjfor's battery into the charger so he would have plenty of battery in case they had to use her when they hunted for Levi's pickup truck.

Trevor shook his head and said that he hoped no additional bodies would be found.

Johnnie said he agreed, and he added that he hoped they would be able to close all the cases. He said he cringed every time he thought about being the parent of one of the missing young women.

Bill suggested they finish the day by searching for the truck.

Johnnie said that he had two additional batteries for Gunjfor, and he hoped that they would be able to locate the truck quickly.

He suggested they drive to someplace close that had a used car lot and hopefully a restaurant where they could get lunch.

Trevor got on his phone and found a nearby highway off the interstate that had several fast-food places and two used car lots.

They agreed that seemed to be a logical place to start their search.

As they turned and drove toward the interstate, Johnnie suggested they stop at the gas station that had a large sign advertising a sit-down restaurant and the best chicken in the world. They all agreed that would be preferable to the fast-food places.

Once they were seated Johnnie leaned back in the booth and said that he felt that after getting control of all of Levi's money and putting it into a trust controlled by Heather's parents, he felt great and for the first time in weeks, he had slept like a baby.

He figured that Alex would figure out how to nail Levy and would get him sent to prison.

There was general agreement that Alex would get him.

After lunch they drove over across the highway to the closest used car lot and after identifying themselves inquired about any recent sales to a rather handsome tall black-haired man.

The lot owner said he hadn't made a sale in a week.

Trevor thanked him and they drove to the second lot where they immediately got a hit.

The lot owner pointed to a lone car sitting on the far corner of the lot. He said he sold one that was similar to the red one, but it was blue and in slightly better condition. They were both scheduled to be taken to auction so he could get them off the lot and he had been happy to make a cash deal with a guy that fit the description that they had given him.

He said that he put on a temporary license plate and signed over the car title. The buyer never gave his name and drove toward the interstate. That was all he knew.

He asked what the guy was wanted for.

"Let's just say he is a bad guy with the police looking for him," Johnnie replied.

The lot owner said that he figured they might have a change to get him if they let the highway patrol know about a blue ford that was putting out a plume of smoke. He added that if the car went over fifty it began to put out lots of smoke.

Johnnie thanked him. He looked around and then asked how far it was to the next small highway or road.

The car dealer commented that about a mile to the east there was a small single lane road that traveled for miles toward the north and passed several smaller farms and then came to an end at a point where the fields became immense. Those fields now blocked the highway. Those huge fields were managed by some big agricultural concern.

Trevor asked if all the smaller farmers were still living on their farms.

The car dealer replied he only knew about one farm that no longer had anyone living on it. It was the one closest to the intersection. Those folks had been married for sixty years and died within two months of each other. He had not known them but had been familiar with an older son who had retired to Florida.

Bill thanked him for the information. He left the car lot and drove toward the intersection in question. He turned onto the one lane black top and drove slowly along the road.

They came to the first driveway and stopped for a moment and then he turned into the gravel road that was beginning to be overgrown by weeds.

Johnnie pointed out the broken weeds in front of the car. He bet that they would find the pickup either in the garage or in the barn.

As the crested a slight hill the saw a two-story red brick house with two loft windows. When they got closer, they saw that all the windows of the house were boarded over and a do not trespass sign was stapled on the front door.

Trevor wondered how many kids the couple might have had and why the farm had not sold.

Bob said he had no idea, but they should act as if Levy was on the property. He stopped in front of the house. He asked if everyone had their vests on. After getting the yeses he was seeking, he took out his weapon and proceeded to the garage. It was locked and sported a do not trespass sign.

He followed as Trevor led the way to the small barn that was across a small field from the house. It had the same do not trespass sign, but the latch mounts had been pulled out of the wood.

He pointed to it. Bob got to one side Johnnie stood behind Trevor as he slowly slid the door open.

They all stepped in and did a quick search and once they were sure Levi was not there, they approached the pickup.

Bob pointed to where three bullets had hit the back window and complemented Johnnie on his shooting. He pointed to a dent in the large black tool chest.

Trevor laughed and said he had found a fifth hit. He pointed to the dent in the center of the rear license plate.

He asked whether Johnnie had been upset and put the last shot between the devil's horns that were on each side of the plate.

Johnnie thanked them for their complements and said he regretted not having a more powerful weapon and no he had not intended to hit the license plate, but the pickup had picked up speed and that was where the last bullet hit.

Bill called Sheriff Milster to let him know that they had located the truck, and it would need to be towed in and put into a secure location until it could be processed.

The Sheriff asked them to wait until a tow truck could get to the pickup to bring it in.

Trevor took pictures of the truck and sent them to the Chief, Alex, and Trey. On the picture of the license plate, he commented that Johnnie was trying to put one between the devil's eyes but had missed the driver.

The Chief texted back and complimented them on finding the truck. He asked about the make of the car that Levi was driving and whether they had any idea where he might be going.

Trevor said the car was a blue fifteen-year-old Ford sedan that was burning oil and gave him the number of the temporary license plate. But they had no clue where it was headed.

After sending the pictures to the Chief, Trevor put his phone in speaker mode and said he was calling Alex to let her know about finding the truck. Alex said that she had just looked at the pictures he had sent. After talking about the car, he added that they had also found another grave.

He then asked if she had any idea of how to figure out where Levi was going.

Alex thought for a moment and asked if there was any way to find out where the family had taken vacations when Levi was younger. She figured that perhaps he would head to a place that he had enjoyed and where he thought he would be safe and hard to find.

Johnnie said that they would look through the house on the farm to see if there were any family albums with pictures. He reminded her that the house had been renovated and he thought maybe even rented out for a while so there might not be anything to find.

After the call and after the tow-truck hauled away the truck, they drove back to the farmhouse to see if they could find an album that had pictures of family vacations.

Trevor smiled and commented that the search blew his idea of getting off from work early. He told Johnnie to be thinking about a great place to have dinner.

Johnnie smiled and said he had one restaurant in mind that was halfway to Cincinnati where they could have a great meal.

The search of the house went faster than expected. The family albums were stored in a sequential series on one bookshelf. Bill found the one that seemed to highlight the earlier years of family get togethers and vacations. It seemed that they had often frequented Lake Cumberland and several other nearby parks with lakes. They agreed that those places were too close.

There were three vacations that included the Grand Canyon, Yellow Stone Park, and a ski vacation in Idaho. Bill held up one picture that had the Levi standing with a lake and mountain view behind it. He turned the picture over and read the inscription that said, "Levi said this was a place where he would like to live." It was dated in a year that would have made Levi about fourteen years old.

Johnnie said that he would do a little digging on the internet to see if he could locate such a place and then share what he had learned with Alex to see what she wanted to do.

He suggested that they call it a day and head toward Cincinnati.

Trevor agreed but then said that he preferred dinner at home.

Bill nodded and agreed with him.

Johnnie simply said, "Ditto."

The day had been trying and long enough for all of them.

13 Long Road West

*L*evi was forced to follow various highways as he made his way west. He now understood why the Interstates had been built. He was traveling through many small towns and along highways that had huge fields either growing corn, soybeans, or alfalfa.

He was nursing his car along and slowly working his way through the case of oil. If he forgot and began to go over sixty a grey burnt oil smelling plum would begin to trail him and let him know. Fifty seemed to be the maximum he could do without burning too much oil.

He figured it would take him a full week to get to where he was going. He thought about his finances and figured he would sleep in his car so that he would have enough money to get a new start when he got to Idaho.

He wished that the radio would work but all he got was a crackling sound from it.

Damn was all that would come to him as he thought about how good his life had been. He was so happy that he had shot and finally killed the Black bitch.

Monday morning the doctor came into Alex's room and said that her lungs were both operating at full capacity, and he was signing the release order. He asked if she had someone to pick her up.

Alex said that she had, and her ride would be at the curb when she got down there.

The doctor wished her a smooth and steady recovery and reminded her to go slow.

A short time after the doctor left the nurse came in and said she was pleased that Alex was recovering. She said she had a message from the nurse that had been shot wishing her all the best and to get the bastard that shot her.

Alex smiled and said that was what she planned to do as soon as possible.

She put in a call to Matt and asked him to meet her at the front of the Hospital. Matt let her know that Johnnie would be driving her car since they had talked and decided not to rent a car or count on the timing of a taxi.

She said that was great and then got dressed in the fresh set of clothes that Matt had brought to her on Sunday. She put the weapon she had been hiding into her shoulder holster she had asked him to bring and then put on her suit jacket. She was ready to go to work.

Johnnie had put on his Ivy Gatsby Newsboy Cabbie Cap and joked with Matt about getting a job being Alex's new chauffer.

Matt laughed and said that he thought his current role as Alex's magician was as high of a position as one could get.

Alex was rolled out in a wheelchair as required by hospital rules but as soon as it stopped rolling, she was up and ready to get in the car. She wished she could go for a long run, but she would be glad to be in at work figuring out how to close the case.

Johnnie tipped his hat as she sat down and in a fake English accent asked where she might be going.

Alex smiled and replied, "please take me home, James."

Johnnie nodded and replied, "as you wish, my fair lass."

Matt shook his head and asked if everyone was having fun.

Alex said that she felt great and that she planned to have a catered lunch at the River Front Park. She wondered if anyone had a specific lunch that they could all enjoy.

Matt called up a menu from a local caterer and they ordered a Greek Salad, a Korean BBQ bowl, a Beef rice bowl, two orders of onion straws and some drinks.

When they arrived, Alex took out the large grey blanket from the trunk and led the way to the area where she had a great view of the river.

After spreading out the blanket, she asked if Johnnie had his computer with him.

Johnnie nodded and said that he did and took it out of a cloth bag that had in it a thick notebook as well. He showed the thick notebook and said that he had decided to carry one after he had realized that a similar one had saved Alex's life.

Alex chuckled and said that she would stand behind him if any shooting started.

Once he had his computer online, she asked if he had figured out where Levi might be going.

Johnnie nodded and said that they had gone through the family photo album and had found one picture of Levi when he was probably about fourteen. The picture was of him with a lake and some mountains behind him. The inscription on the back said that this was a place that he wished he could live.

The other pictures were in a campground somewhere in or near Yellow Stone.

Johnnie said he was betting on the location of the lake. He had run a picture recognition routine and had a hit on a lake that seemed to have the same background.

Alex asked where the lake was located.

Johnnie pulled up a map and showed Alex a view of the mountains near Coeur d'Alene.

Alex said that she was going to put out an APB warrant with instructions to notify her if the car was spotted but to track and not arrest.

She called the Chief and asked him if he would set it up and that she did not want Levi arrested but only tracked she wanted to capture him and bring him back to Ohio so they would not have to go through an extradition process.

The Chief agreed with her adding that he wanted the trial to be quick and to be in Cincinnati.

The lunch arrived and Alex concentrated on getting a taste of each lunch item, sipping on her tea, and enjoying the onion straws. She was thinking about how to get ahead of Levi.

She asked if Johnnie had seen any logs going down the river.

Johnnie shook his head in the negative and said he had been too busy defending his Korean BBQ from her to look for logs.

Alex apologized and handed him her Beef rice bowl and said he could have it.

Johnnie shook his head and said she had already contaminated it and he would just have to be satisfied with what he had.

Alex studied the shapes of the clouds floating slowly by high in the light blue sky and was almost falling asleep when her phone rang. She answered and listened as the Chief let her know that they had a hit on a secondary highway near Dickinson Montana of an old blue Ford sedan clearly burning oil with an Iowa license plate. It was heading toward the Idaho border at about fifty miles per hour.

Alex commented that the Iowa license plate made sense. Levi had probably replaced the temporary one with one he took off of some car.

The Chief asked what she was thinking about doing.

She replied that she was thinking about a field trip. She would need an arrest warrant, and flight tickets to Idaho.

Alex asked if Trey was in the office.

The Chief said that Trey was in. He added that he would arrange to get the flight tickets for the two of them and he would have the arrest warrant by the time Trey was ready to go to the airport.

Alex thanked him and said that she would likely stop by the office on the way to the airport.

She sat up and said that lunch was over, and she needed to get ready for a field trip.

Matt shook his head and said that she had only one speed and that was full speed ahead. He helped up and said he hoped that she was flying first class so she could rest during the flight.

Alex smiled, gave him a kiss, and agreed but that in each case she always knew that she was getting a bad guy off the street.

Johnnie smiled and said that she should just shoot this guy and get it over with.

Alex agreed that would be appropriate, but she would only do so if he resisted arrest and took another shot at her.

When Johnnie drove into the parking lot, Trey was standing on the curb by the side entrance to the station.

Johnnie dropped Alex off and then parked the car at the very back of the lot where Alex always parked. He walked up to the two and said he was going to walk home.

Johnnie was walking away when the taxi came into the lot. He watched as Trey helped Alex into the car. He figured that Trey would make sure she took it as easy as he could.

Once they were on the way, Trey said that Nolan had wanted her to know that he expected her to get the bad guy but that she should be sure to wear her Kevlar vest.

Alex smiled and said she had her spare along and would follow Nolan's advice.

Trey nodded and then added that Lesley had simply said they should be safe and watch each other's back.

Alex verified they had the right paperwork and were ready to make the arrest.

The flight out was long but the treatment in first class was superb. Alex ate a banana and then went to sleep. She knew that she was not yet in top shape.

Upon landing they went to the car rental and picked up the SUV that had been reserved for them and then drove out of the airport.

They had landed at the airport closest to Coeur d'Alene, but it was actually in Oregon. They drove across the border into Idaho.

It was a short drive back to their destination. It gave them a magnificent view of the Rocky Mountains towering high into the puffy clouds that seemed to be hugging the peaks.

The Chief called them and said that the Idaho police had followed Levi to a campground near the eastern end of Lake Coeur d'Alene. He gave her the location and told her to take care.

He gave her a phone number and said that this was the person who would be with her when she made the arrest and would be a witness at the trial if it was necessary.

Alex thanked him and verified that she had a return ticket for Levi.

The Chief assured her that she did, and it was in first Class next to Trey.

Alex made the call and arranged to meet a Brigham Slayen, Sheriff of Coeur d'Alene. He asked where they should meet. She suggested a lunch spot of his choosing.

She put the address he gave her into maps and settled back as Trey drove. She closed her eyes and relaxed.

He looked over at her and asked if she was going to try and get back to Cincinnati on the same day.

Alex nodded and said that she figured a redeye would have seats available.

They met the Sheriff and after greetings he said that the restaurant was rather new, but it had great food. He suggested they sit outside and enjoy the sun. After they sat down, he said that he often ate at this restaurant and had tried both the fish and the meat, and both were superb. He added that the signature desert was to die for.

Alex smiled and said that she had to be awake when she made the arrest.

After the orders had been put in, the Sheriff asked whether this person was dangerous and what he was being arrested for.

Alex said that the arrest warrant was for the attempted murder of a police officer.

The Sheriff asked how that officer was doing.

Alex smiled and said she was doing fine.

The Sheriff said he was glad to hear that. He would certainly not want this guy in his jurisdiction.

Alex said she agreed with him and hoped to arrest him early in the afternoon.

She asked if he had body armor to use during the arrest.

The Sheriff smiled and said that he wished he did, but the budget had never been big enough for any of his guys to have anything but a bullet proof shield.

Alex nodded and asked him to use his shield.

The Sheriff looked at her and asked if she was serious.

Alex nodded and said she was.

The order came and she sliced through one of the lamb chops and was delighted with how it was done and how the cranberry sauce enhanced its flavor.

She asked Trey to split the desert she had ordered and smiled when he said that he had counted on that and had passed up ordering one for himself.

The Sheriff asked how long they had been partners.

Alex smiled and said that the partnership was not in years, but it was over several lifetimes.

The Sheriff stopped as he took a bite of his desert. He looked at her and then asked if she was known as "Cincinnati's Black Annie Oakley."

Alex nodded and said that was a moniker that would follow her for her lifetime.

The Sheriff let out a "Wow" exclamation and said that his wife and daughter were constantly talking about her and how she was inspiring young women to do what had always been forbidden by society for them to do.

They pointed out the fact that that she had a law degree but had chosen to become a cop instead of a lawyer.

Alex smiled and said that she was honored to be thought of that way. She said that she had simply decided that getting the bad guy to be judged by a jury of his peers was a role that she preferred.

The Sheriff said that he wanted to get a picture with her because his wife and daughter would never believe him when he shared who he was having lunch with.

Alex handed Trey her phone and asked him to take a picture of the Sheriff and her.

After lunch Alex suggested they all drive out to the campground but go in on foot. She said she hoped not to scare any of the people camping.

She verified that the Sheriff had his shield in his trunk.

He said that he did and asked where her shield was.

Alex pulled her jacket back and said she was wearing hers.

The drive out took about twenty minutes. It was about three in the afternoon on a sunny but cool day with a light breeze that was coming across the lake. It was the type of weather anyone that camped cherished and enjoyed.

They parked behind a police car that was already there.

The Sheriff introduced one of his deputies who let them know that the car that they were looking for was parked six campgrounds back into the park.

As she led the way in Alex was impressed. The camps were separated by lush green grass and a bed of lavender stone crop flowers along the front edge of each green area. It made the campground seem like a small paradise by the lake.

She hoped that they could capture Levi without a gun fight.

Had Levi known that he was about to be arrested he might have had his weapons ready instead it was laying by his side, and he was daydreaming about his new life in the west. He had already seen several potential new skulls earlier when he had walked around the campground.

He figured it was too early to harvest but it didn't hurt to look. He figured he would see if he could find a farm that needed help. He was betting on locating an old couple on some out of the way farm. Life would once again be good.

Alex indicated that the Sheriff should stay in the lane, the deputy should go to the lake side of the car and she and Trey would approach the car.

She slowly approached the driver's side and Trey took the other side. She was crouched down by the rear door when she gave the signal and they both opened the back doors at the same time.

Levi looked up and bolted out of the door and knocked Alex down all the time screaming that it was not possible. He had his gun in hand and turned to run away from all of them.

Trey ran around the front and hit Levi from the side and the two of them slid across the grass parallel to the border of the flower bed.

Trey hit him once with the flat of his hand across his mouth, flipped him over, put the handcuffs on and pulled him to his feet and read him his Miranda rights.

The Sheriff's deputy put the gun into the evidence bag.

Levi was still blubbering about the fact that he had killed her and that it was not possible.

Alex walked up to him smiled and let him know that she had a deal with the devil that let her stay alive if she sent guys like him down as a gift.

She looked at the sheriff and asked if there was a holding cell she could borrow and if he could arrange to have the car taken to a secure holding area because she was sure there would be evidence that need to be processed. She said that she was specifically looking for a high-powered rifle.

The Sheriff said that her request would be no problem. He gave instructions to his deputy and then said that they should all head to the station. He would take the perp back in his car.

Levi seemed to have gone over the edge. He kept mumbling and repeating that she had a deal with the devil.

Once back in the station Alex made a call to the Chief and let him know that they had Levi and had been able to do it without a gunfight. She asked to see if the Chief's support would arrange for a redeye special back to Cincinnati.

When the Sheriff heard the request for the flight back, he said that she would have several hours waiting, and would it be possible to ask that his daughter and wife could have dinner with her.

Alex said that dinner would be fine, but she needed a nap before then and asked if there was a cot available.

The Chief asked if she was the one that the perp had shot.

Alex said that he had hit her once and had tried a second time to kill her when she was in the hospital.

The Sheriff said he had just the place for her to take her nap and made a call.

He then told Trey to follow him.

Alex was surprised to enter a neighborhood that bordered a golf course and then have the sheriff pull into a double wide driveway and park.

Trey pulled up beside him and they all got out.

Alex smiled as the Sheriff welcomed her to his humble abode. She knew that he was proud of his abode, and it was far from humble.

His wife and daughter rushed out.

The Sheriff introduced them and stepped back.

Alex was surprised to be pulled into a group hug by his wife and daughter. She gave a small laugh of surprise as she was gushed over as they said it was like a dream come true that they would be able to meet her and have dinner with her.

Then she was pulled in and taken to the guest bedroom for her nap.

14 Body Forty-Three

*T*he flight home provided Alex with time to reflect. She had captured one of the most horrific individuals in a small town in Idaho where she was treated as a heroine by a family who admired her. She was going to get back the day after having left and would be able to sleep in her own bed.

She had ended up eating a catered dinner at the Sheriff's house.

She learned that Trey had suggested it and they had ordered from the same restaurant where they had lunch. He let her know that he had ordered the steak she had mentioned during lunch as her second choice, and he had ordered a lamb roast in case she did not want the steak.

The dinner conversation centered on what the Sheriff's daughter was thinking about majoring in when she went to college. When asked for her suggestion Alex had suggested going for a degree that would allow her to have a good income in a field that seemed to hold the potential for a good life.

Once she was into that field, she should see what doors were open for her to make her life fulfilling and go for it.

On the way to the airport the Sheriff stopped at the border and said that his jurisdiction ended at the border and transferred custody of Levi to her. He presented her with a golf bag that he said had the rifle and the gun inside and handed her the paperwork that would allow her to check it in.

He thanked her for the advice she had given to his daughter.

Alex and Trey got to the airport and once at the gate had let Levi know that they would be flying first class, but he would have his ankles chained to the seat and would not be allowed up.

He nodded and agreed to let Trey take him into the men's room before boarding.

Every time Levi looked at her, he would mumble something about the devil, or the witch and he deal she had.

During the flight, Alex thought about the case. She had survived another attack on her life. But what bothered her the most was of the very grotesque nature of the case that would leave forty-two families devastated for the rest of their lives. She would recover and would continue to seek out the bad guys, but she knew there was no end to bad guys whether they were men or women. It gave her the chills sitting next to a person that looked like any other person but had a mind so warped that he had methodically hunted for, killed, and beheaded all those young women.

It was a redeye flight but there was no way she would fall asleep. Earlier she had instructed Levi to be quiet when he kept asking how she had survived. He had finally complied when she asked the flight attendant if she had any duct tape.

Trey was a little cruder and told Levi he would break his jaw.

For the rest of the flight Levi merely mumbled to himself.

Alex was relieved when the pilot announced they would soon land. It had been one of the most uncomfortable flights she had so far taken.

She was more relieved when she got on the up escalator to baggage claim and looked up and saw Bill and Trevor.

The two greeted them and said that they were there to take all of them back to the station. After retrieving the luggage, they took Levi between them and led the way out to the black panel van, and they all got in. There were two policemen in the front two seats and the five of them sat in the back.

Bill let her know that the Chief had told her to go fishing or to do whatever she wished but that she should not come into work.

Alex replied that what she wished was to get some sleep and she was planning to do that as soon as she got to her apartment.

Trey said he was going home and do the same.

Bill volunteered to take him home since he lived close by.

Trey thanked him and said that would be great.

After being dropped off Alex went to her apartment, stood under the hot shower, and let all the tension melt away. As she dried off, she decided to make a call before getting into her bed.

She dialed John Williams and asked him to take the Levi's case when it came time to formally charge him. She asked that he make sure that the judge did not allow bail and would put Levi in prison until his case came before a jury.

She then wrote a quick text to Matt letting him know she was home and getting some sleep.

She did not wake up until some twelve hours later. She felt much better but took a pill to reduce the pain she had in the center of her chest.

A few days later she was sitting in the court room as Levi was arraigned. The judge had been appraised about the horrific nature of the charges. John had Brian Lexter, the Cincinnati FBI bureau chief, describe the excavation of forty-two graves that was going on at the farm formally owned by Levi.

The lawyer for the defense corrected Brian and said that the defendant still owned the property. John objected and said that he had checked the facts and that a Linda and Arnold Preston now owned the property that the defendant Levi Misle had put into their deceased daughter's trust.

Levi looked over at her and she returned a smile and a nod.

He said something to his lawyer and then looked down at his hands on the table. He knew he was screwed by the witch that made deals with the devil.

The defense withdrew the objection.

The judge ruled that Levi would be held in a high security prison without bail until he was brought back to stand trial.

She banged her gavel and declared the court session was over.

Alex was walking out the door with the Chief when the judge stopped to congratulate the Chief on getting the case closed so quickly. She did not look at Alex but said that she was pleased to have her bring another bad guy before her and looked forward to many more. She added that she was very biased against this latest person and was glad to see that Alex had worked her devil's magic.

It was clear to Alex that the judge was speaking to her but did not want the public to know. The two of them knew each other well.

Alex smiled but remained quiet.

The Chief stood for a minute as the Judge walked away. He looked at Alex and told her he did not want to know anything about the devil's magic.

Alex was about to walk away when John and Hanna walked out of the building and said they were going to their favorite coffee shop to celebrate getting Levi locked up for good.

She accepted and asked the Chief if he wanted to join in.

The Chief said he would be going back to his office and that Alex had the rest of the day off.

Once they were in the coffee shop and had placed their order, John thanked her for giving him the information about the property transfer. He did not want to know how she had gotten the records changed but he let her know that he had his team check out all the paperwork and they had let him know that all signatures on the transfer paperwork were authentic and were Levi's.

She took a sip of her latte and smiled, nodded, and replied that she had a magician working for her.

She thought about her meeting with Linda and Arnold Preston. She had put them in charge of a ten-million-dollar trust named after their daughter that would give each of the forty-two parents twelve thousand dollars a year for the rest of their lives. And then the trust would be available to the future generations of those families.

They had welcomed the opportunity and had accepted the financial institution's offer to manage the account for them.

She looked up from her latte as she realized she was daydreaming and asked John and Hann if the two of them would like to take part in a bike ride that she and Matt were going to take with his team on the following morning.

They thanked her but declined because both of them had cases in full swing and that they needed to keep on track.

Early the next morning, Trey and his team took off along the river front. Alex and Johnnie were at the rear. They were both riding the bikes that had been impounded during their last case when they had been shot at by three would be killers that together they killed. It had taken months to get the bikes released and then Alex's bike needed to have the front wheel replaced and the back wheel straightened.

They had laughed about the fact that the bike took longer than her to get back into shape.

Alex enjoyed the day as she realized what a great team Matt had working with him. They had repeatedly been the team that had either shown up and supported her or had taken her to the hospital and were instrumental several times in saving her. The ride was a resounding success and she felt great that she was once again back to her normal physical form.

The day after the bike ride the Chief called her into his office. He said he had just gotten off the phone with the head of the high security prison that Levi had been sent to. He asked if she had anything to do with what had happened there.

Alex looked at him and said that she had no idea what he was talking about.

He nodded and let her know that Levi had been killed during an outdoor ball game at the prison. He was the pitcher for the winning team. The players from both teams ran to the pitcher's mound and surrounded Levi as if to celebrate.

When the prisoners moved away, the guards saw that Levi's head had been cut off and his head was being held up on a broken baseball bat planted in the ground and the number forty-three had been scratched into the dirt on the mound.

The Chief said that somehow the prisoners had learned who Levi was and imposed their own justice.

Alex shook her head. She said that she had nothing to do with it and she was sure that her team would not have done anything like it.

She said that she and her team focused on bringing the bad guy to face the judge and be judged by a jury of his peers.

The Chief nodded and reassured her that he was sure no one in his department would have leaked the information. He added that he was not going to assign any resources to figure out who had because he could think of nothing better than for Levi to have been treated as he had treated so many other innocent women.

Alex walked out of the office knowing that it was someone who had somehow learned of the situation and there was a short list of those "someones" and it would be quite easy to find out who. She planned to have Johnnie make that list hard to find.

She knew that she would sleep much easier knowing that Levi was down with the devil he had served.

The End

Preview of: The Vanishing

1 Comacho

A red bandana hugged the head of the person handing a small package to the person who in turn was passing a hand full of cash back to his other hand. This was a scene being repeated in numerous dark corners or alleys throughout the city. Business was booming and Comacho controlled a lucrative part of the drug distribution business. He was not the biggest distributor. He was one of the toughest and in control of his distribution area, and he was raking in the money. He purposely kept a low profile and maintained good relations with his competitors by agreeing to the territory in which he distributed, and he gave a small cut of the take to keep the good relations greased. His adversaries also were very aware of his ruthlessness.

He knew he was destined to go to hell. He figured he might be able to pal around with the Devil. He planned to continue to be ruthless and to control those who worked for him.

He had grown up as one of the Reds and had learned that strength and ruthlessness were the ingredients that let one survive in the harsh environment that he had been raised in.

He had no patience with those who hesitated to do as he commanded. He had personally shot and killed more than a dozen men and women. Yes women! They demanded equal treatment, and he gladly gave it to them. He had no patience for insubordination. When he ordered something, he expected immediate follow-through, and he usually got it.

There were two ways he handled those he decided to eliminate.

Regular offenders who would not pay out or distributors that encroached on his territory were taken care of by his hirelings.

For those more egregious offenders he had a special ceremony that he personally orchestrated. He would have a fifty-gallon barrel filled three quarters of the way with a chemical that was heavy on lye, and he would have his nude victim placed feet first into the barrel. Then he would ask the screaming individual to ask him to shoot and kill them. When they asked him to shoot, he would but he would shoot that person in the arm. Then he would ask the screaming individual to tell him where he should shoot. Often the request was in the head, sometimes through the heart. But he would not do it until he made the person say, "Please shoot me in the ---." Often the legs of the individual would give out and he had to be held in the vertical position.

Once the individual was dead, he left the area after giving instructions to sink the body into the drum and then seal it.

The drum was filled to the very brim before sealing it so it would sink like a rock. He had the drum taken out to sea and ensured it would sink by adding additional weight to it.

Only one woman had suffered that fate. She was an assassin hired by a competitor drug dealer. She had been the toughest of the twelve that had stood in the barrel. When he asked her where he should shoot her, she had screamed "put the bullet in your head" and she had then she crouched down into the barrel and put her head under the chemical bath.

He had been amazed by her toughness she had not started to scream when placed into the barrel! He almost regretted that she had tried to kill him. He figured she might have been his soul mate. A vile soul mate from hell. "Oh, well," he laughed as he thought about the Devil sending him a message.

He decided to kill the drug dealer that had hired her, to see if he would be as tough as she had been. He was not. He cried and screamed like a baby.

Ironically, the word got out about his having eliminated the female assassin and the drug dealer and he was charged with murder. He of course pleaded innocent. The problem for the prosecutor was that he did not have a body and was operating on hearsay. His lawyer and the prosecutor reached an agreement that if he left the state the case would be dropped.

He set up his second in command to run the drug distribution business. He wanted thirty per cent of the take to be sent to an offshore account.

He had no plans to stop distributing so he looked around to see where in the country he would set himself up.

He figured he needed to find a low-profile location but one that was well positioned geographically in the drug trade.

He looked north to Seattle and decided that it was not well located.

He looked to Chicago but realized that the battle between the Mafia and the Mexican cartels would put him in the middle between two powerful and deadly groups. That situation eliminated Chicago.

New York City was out because of the state's focus on rooting out drug distributors. It would make it hard to carve out distribution territory.

He went down the list of the large cities in the east and eliminated all of them.

He looked at the US map and realized that one central point in the drug distribution was the city that had been described by one New Yorker as, "the sleepy little city by the Ohio River." He moved the arrow on the screen and made a circle around Cincinnati.

He bought a one-way first-class plane ticket to Cincinnati.

He had his Mercedes-Benz SL Cabriolet driven there so that he would have his favorite car to use.

He spent a few days in Cincinnati in a luxury downtown hotel suite while he explored the city on foot. He walked the Ohio Riverfront Park. He located the police station and walked all around that area.

He found the place he was looking for. It was a bar about three blocks away from the police station. He walked in and asked the current owner what he wanted for the place.

The owner asked why he would want a place that did not do much business. He said that he was ready to sell but didn't want to unload a dying bar. He gave a price of what he thought the building and property was worth and said that he currently was breaking even on the business. He asked again why he would want to buy the business.

Camacho replied that it seemed to be located in a place close to the downtown area but out of the beaten path. He agreed to the asking price but wanted six months' time before he needed to make the payment.

He then asked who the regular customers happened to be and was not surprised to learn that there were several cops that frequented the place. He hoped that one of them would be open to a little extra cash for inside information about what was coming down. He also needed to make sure the regular cops were willing to look the other way to the traffic of distributors that might be entering and leaving the bar.

He made it a point to be friendly with all of the cops that came in and slowly figured out which one was most likely to be susceptible to making a lucrative arrangement and would agree to be an inside informant.

When that policeman's bar bill began to build up, he made his proposal. The policeman thought he was a great bargainer and bargained for free drinks as a part of such an arrangement. Comacho figured that a bottle of booze a week was a very cheap bribe and he added that if he got the information that he requested he would sweeten the arrangement. He figured that he could keep the monetary honey at a low level.

His early requests were simple and information he could get himself, but it provided a way to get the informant relaxed and willing to share information. The first thing he asked about was the number of high schools inside the two seventy-five loop. He figured the roughly twenty-five that he got an address for would be about the right number to set up a lucrative and low-key drug distribution network.

It was time to set up a small local distribution organization. He reached back to his L.A. network and got the names of three individuals that he could hire. One was located in Cincinnati; one was from L.A. who had worked for him there and one was from the Columbus area. He figured the mix would give him a small group that had the moxie to run the operation. He hired the three and assigned them the role of recruiting drug distributors at each of the high schools and distributing the drugs to them.

He gave them the profile of a good high school drug distributor. The individual had to be a person that demonstrated being a leader but who was either a loner or an individual who bullied others.

It could be a female but most often would probably be a male. He or she would stand out during the morning when school started and during the end of the day rush out of the school. He or she could be of any race. The poorer the better. However, they could not be on any drugs to be a distributor.

The individual would be given a starting bonus and initially five percent of the sales income.

He let the three who would be doing the recruiting know that they would each get five percent of the drugs their high school distributors sold so they should make sure to coach them and give them some additional rewards like free meals or rides to social events. In other words, set up a positive relationship with these young distributors. Finally, they should be setting up the next person to take the place of a high schooler that was graduating.

Setting up the distribution network and getting a local drug production facility established took him about six months. He was lucky and found an abandoned fire station just across town that he was able to lease. He imported a druggist from L.A. and set him up in the station. He funded the operation but stayed well away from what he figured was a group of druggies making more drugs.

He was able to buy a large home with several acres on the east side of the city that was only about fifteen minutes from the bar where he would have his operational office.

He felt good about the transition. Cincinnati did not have the nightlife that was available in L.A., but it featured a variety of engaging theatrical plays, orchestra performances, boating on nearby lakes and on the Ohio River. He figured he would enjoy a quieter lifestyle and become more active outdoors.

<u>*2 The Vanishing*</u>

*T*he hallway was a maze of students weaving around each other, talking in small groups, or yelling to friends. There were also confrontations between some students and consistently three bullies would corner some person but most often some young female that they would harass.

Jesse navigated his way down the crowded hall as he hastened to make it to his next class. He had just escaped another scrimmage with these three bullies who were his nemesis. He was being hounded because he had interceded when the three had cornered a reluctant female student. The three were recognized throughout the school as bullies. He also suspected them of being the school's drug suppliers. He was certain they were connected to the Red Bandana gang that controlled the drug distribution in the area. This worried him because he knew that the gang was violent and would corner a person when they were alone.

It was Saturday morning, and he was on the way to buy a new pair of basketball shoes. He spotted a young woman being harassed.

He should have minded his own business, but she was getting attacked by these three mean looking dudes wearing red bandanas. He shouted at them to stop and when they turned to respond to him the lady dashed away.

He took off but they caught up with him. When they caught up with him, he realized they were the three bullies that often pushed him around at school. He knew he was in big trouble.

They began pounding on him and said they were going to beat him to death. He fought as best as he could, but he took a brutal beating. It only stopped when a police car came driving by and turned on its red lights.

He used that moment, like the young woman, to dash away but he heard one of the bully's shout at him that they were not through with him or anyone else in his family.

The image of his sister came to his mind. His sister, April, was only fifteen and was a freshman. She was excited about beginning high school. She was doing well in her classes, was a junior varsity cheer leader and had a minor role in one of the theatrical school plays.

He adored April. He figured if he vanished from the scene, the three hoods would move on, and she would be alright. This was all he could think of as he ran seemingly in a random direction.

That had been earlier in a grey cloud covered day that deteriorated into a continuous drizzle that had seemed determined to make him cold and miserable.

His sweatshirt was soaked and the only reason he kept it on was because even in the wet condition it was keeping him warm.

He pulled his hood tight trying to keep the drizzle out. The day had faded into a night as dark as the thoughts in his mind. He found himself walking eastward but he had no clue where he was going. The blood had stopped running from his nose and the drizzle seemed to be keeping it moistened. His other cuts had all crusted over. He was a mess. He would need to find a place where he could wash up so he would be somewhat presentable. He felt lucky to have escaped alive.

The beating had been almost eight hours ago. The rumble in his stomach gave him a blunt unadulterated reality check about his current situation. He was wet, he was hungry, and he had no place to stop to get some sleep.

He had just made the basketball team and that morning he had emptied his money box so he could buy a new pair of Nike basketball shoes. That money was in his backpack. The idea of buying the Nike shoes was now history. That money had to last until he could get to wherever he was going, and until he got paid for the job, a job that he knew he needed to get.

He wondered if he had enough cash to carry him through until he had a job and a first paycheck. He thought about how his mother stretched her paycheck to make sure she always had food for the family. She always bought fifty-pound bags of rice and beans, large jars of peanut butter, of strawberry jam and grape jelly, and day-old loaves of bread.

She made a point of letting him and April know that chicken, ham, and any other meat was a treat and would be cooked sparingly.

He figured that he would have to copy what she did when shopping so he could stretch the money he had in the backpack.

He looked ahead and saw a large honeysuckle bush growing under a railway overpass. He crawled under it and got as close to the trunk of the bush as possible and made himself as comfortable as he could. He would have liked to take off his wet sweatshirt, but the night was already cold to him. He hoped that it would be sunny the next day so he could dry off.

He felt like death warmed over, was miserable but he finally fell asleep.

The morning sun woke him up and the clear blue cloudless sky gave his down feelings a lift. He took off his sweatshirt and hung it from his backpack. His long sleeve shirt was damp to the touch, but it soon dried off as he walked.

He was on one of the smaller highways going east across Ohio. The occasional car or pickup went by, but none stopped to offer him a ride. As a Black man he did not expect to get picked up. He took long strides and kept walking.

Just about the time he was about to give up on getting to somewhere where he could get something to eat, he came up over a hill and saw that down in the valley, there was a small one street village hugging the banks of a small river.

Tall old oaks and maples provided a shading canopy for most of the buildings in town. They appeared to be the barrier that kept the weeping willows along the river at bay. As he approached the town, it was as if he had stepped back in time. He half expected to see gunslingers and horses.

He saw only one store that had a sign advertising that they were a hardware and grocery. He entered and was greeted by an older lady sitting on a tall stool who asked him how she could be of help.

He asked if she had any sandwiches or something that he could have for a late breakfast. She led the way to the back of the store where there was a large coffee pot, a microwave and small freezer that had a variety of sandwiches and other microwaveable offerings.

She let him know that a cup of coffee and any one selection from the freezer was five dollars.

After looking over the selection, he chose a mac and cheese package because it was the largest amount of food.

After wolfing down the food he walked around the small grocery section and selected a two-pound bag of rice and a large bag of dry black beans. He then found a small metal pan that he figured he would use to cook with. Finally, he picked up a large bottle of water.

He took everything to the counter where, as his selection was being rung up, the lady asked where he was going.

He answered that he was not sure but somewhere along the East Coast.

She smiled and let him know that in the next town he would be able to catch a bus. She then let him know that breakfast was on her and wished him good luck.

He thanked her for being so kind and then paid her with some of his precious cash.

He then went on his way. Now he was thinking about where on the East Coast he would go, and he wondered if he had enough money to buy the ticket and still have enough left over so he could last until he landed a job.

In the next town he located the bus station. He was surprised that he could go to almost anywhere along the East Coast for about one hundred dollars.

He felt a sense of relief that he would have enough money left over for food, but he would need to figure out where to sleep at night. He was sure that he would not be able to stay in any hotel or motel.

After considering the cities along the coast, he chose Virginia Beach as the place that he would try to establish himself. He was not at all sure why he had selected it, but it seemed to be the halfway point between going north or going south.

The bus ride gave him time to get some sleep, think through what he would do so he could feed himself and where he might be able to find a place where he could sleep.

He figured he would have to locate a homeless shelter and hope that he would get the help he needed to find a job and an affordable place to live.

The bus arrived early in the morning. Once again, his stomach was growling. He walked out of the bus station and looked around. He saw an old Black guy pushing a cart filled with bottles and tin cans.

He walked over to him and asked if he knew where a person could get something to eat at no cost.

The old guy looked at him and told him he was too young to become a beggar and should get a job.

Jesse nodded and asked him where he might find a job.

The old guy smiled and said that he should go to the Mayfair Home of Hope where he could get a good meal and while he was there, he should see if they could point him to a job. He added that it would not be a job being the president of some company, but it would let him make enough to let him eat. He pointed at his cart and said that his other option was to collect bottles and cans and take them to the recycling center where he would get about two cents per bottle and a penny a can. He added that he covered the territory for blocks around and would fight him off.

Jesse thanked him for the information and asked for directions to the Home of Hope.

The old man pointed in the direction opposite to the one he was going and said that it was about seven blocks. He said good luck and continued on his way.

Jesse took up a brisk walk and he soon saw the sign outside a building that looked like it might once have been an apartment building.

He read the sign on the outside of the building that said it gave food, comfort, and the opportunity to start anew.

He figured that he qualified and that he was certainly starting new.

He walked up the steps and entered.

He was greeted by a gray bearded person that looked like an anemic Santa Claus. He was asked what he needed.

Jesse let it all flow out, "something to eat, a place to sleep and a job."

The old guy said that he was in luck and would be able to get a tray of food before the breakfast line closed to get ready for the noon meal. He told Jesse to get his tray of food and while he was eating a social worker would come out to ask him a few questions.

Jessi went in, grabbed a tray, and went down the line.

There was only one server who smiled and put huge helpings on the tray. He commented that normally he should not expect so much but it had been a slow morning. The server put two apples and two bananas on the counter and said he should take them as well.

Jessi could hardly carry the tray to the nearest table. He looked around and realized he was one of five people in the cafeteria.

He was famished and dug in. The scrambled eggs, the three patties of sausage, and a large blue berry muffin disappeared.

He went over to a large coffee pot and poured himself a cup and put in three creamers and carried it back to his table to finish a sugar covered cake donut. He planned to eat the bananas and apples later.

An older Black woman approached and introduced herself as Renee and let him know that she was a registered nurse and psychologist, and she had a few questions to ask him.

Jesse nodded and waited for the questions.

The first question was about his age, then what level of education he had and then what job experience he had.

She reacted to his age and said that he looked older than eighteen. Then she asked why he had not finished high school.

Jesse said that he had to run because he had crossed wires with the local drug dealer, and they had threatened to kill him and had almost succeed. He opened his shirt to show the bruises that were now turning yellow.

He then listened as Renee said that he was in luck, and she would be able to take him in and get him an interview at a local restaurant as a bus boy. The pay would not be enough to enable him to rent a room somewhere so he might need to get a second job. However, he would have a couple months to get the second job and to find a place to live.

She asked if he wanted to finish getting his high school diploma.

Jesse said getting a high school diploma would be great and would give him the chance to try and go on to college.

Renee smiled and said that she liked his attitude and said that he would be shown to his room, and he should get oriented. She added that there would be no cooking in the room. If he had a hot plate, he should not think about using it.

She told him that he should be ready to go at eight the next morning. She was going to make a couple of calls and get a job interview lined up.

Once in his room, he got oriented. It had a shower, a bar of soap, and some towels. He decided to take a shower and wash his t-shirt, drawers and socks and put them in the sunlight to dry. He wrapped the towel around his waist and lay down on the bed. The mattress was a hard one that he thought was just what he needed.

He went to sleep wondering how he would wake up to get to breakfast and be ready by eight.

A blasting horn in the hallway at six in the morning brough him wide awake. He now knew that he would not have to buy an alarm clock.

He got up and went to the sink, opened the medicine cabinet, and found a comb, a toothbrush, and a tube of toothpaste. He brushed his teeth, spruce up, got dressed in his still damp clothes and went down the stairs to the cafeteria.

By six thirty he had a tray in hand and went down the breakfast line and selected the over easy eggs, some sausage, two pieces of toast and two patties of butter. He added a carton of milk and took a banana. He looked around and realized he was one of the first people in the cafeteria.

Renee came over to his table and gave him a card with the person at the restaurant that would be expecting him, and that the restaurant was a twelve-block walk.

Jesse asked for the directions and Renee handed him a piece of paper with a hand drawn map on it.

He thanked her for getting him an interview so quickly. He added that he hoped to come back and let her know that he had a job.

He left right after breakfast and after a brisk walk arrived thirty minutes early. He let the breakfast host know he had come for a job interview.

He was asked to wait at the entrance. He watched the people arriving and realized he was definitely in a white neighborhood.

The manager came out and led him to a table in the back corner where he offered him something to drink.

He said that the water would be fine.

The grey-haired white manager appeared to him to be in his late forties or maybe early fifties. He was clearly overweight and seemed out of shape.

He asked a few questions and then asked him to sign a paper that would let the restaurant to check his background. He then offered a busboys job, one meal each day, the minimum hourly rate of pay plus a share of the tips.

Jesse accepted and asked when he could begin.

The manager replied that it could be immediately and asked Jesse to follow him.

About the Author

Ronald E. Mueller
remwriter95@gmail.com

Ron grew up in what is now Flint River State Park in Southeast Iowa. The 170-year-old house Ron lived in is built into a hillside. It faces a 125-foot-high cliff towering over the little Flint River. The house and the land talked to him about; the passing of time, the struggle to conquer the land, the struggles people faced and the wonder of nature.

He climbed the cliffs, crawled into the caves, dove from the swimming rock, collected clams from the bottom of the pond, gigged and skinned frogs for their legs. He trapped muskrats for fur, hunted raccoon in the dead of night, and with only a stick hunted rabbits in the dead of winter.

His young life was outdoors, and nature tested him.

He walked to a one room stone schoolhouse uphill both ways. A stern but warm-hearted teacher, Mrs. Henry was instrumental in shaping his character as she shepherded him from the fourth to the eighth grade.

It was a great way to grow up.

Ron graduated from Burlington, High School, went to Vietnam in the Navy. He graduated from The University of South Florida with a master's degree in engineering, worked for thirty eight years for Procter and Gamble, traveled around the world thirty times.

He has remained happily married for more than fifty years. His daughter and his two sons are all successful and his three grandchildren have all graduated.

His wife has humored and supported him as he became a full time professional story teller.

He has come to realize that he is, what is known as, a Cozy writer. Excitement and adventure but little guts and gore. His heroine or hero suffer a little but live happily ever after.

His experiences inter-twined with snippets of fantasy lend themselves to the adventures he leads the reader through.

<u>**Science Fiction**</u>

The Savitar Series
Journey's End
Savitar
Confluence
Savitar Series Collection

The Door Series
The Door
Aliens We
The Endless Hole
The Swarm
Esoteric Journey
The Gentle Eye
The Door Series Collection

Bram Nielson Series
The Fold
The Message
Fold Wormhole
Negative Fold
Ripples in Time
Bram Nielson Collection

<u>**Single Science Fiction Books:**</u>
Current Past and Future
The Event
The Door
Viajante 7

Characters in the Story

Characters in the Story

Alex	Cathy	Evercrest	Police Detective
Matthew	Timothy	Knolton	Alex's suitor
Rose-Anne	Germain	Evercrest	Alex's mother
Russel	Johnson	Evercrest	Alex's father
Helping Hands charity			Alex's nonprofit org
Trey		McGregor	Alex's Detective Partner
Lindsey		McGregor	Wife
Nolan		McGregor	Son
Johnnie		Smith	Old Viet Vet
Mary		Higgins	Johnnie's Phili "friend"
Bruce	Lincoln	Johnson	Cinci Chief of Detectives
Mary-Anne	Leslie	Johnson	Chiefs Wife
Bill	Hamilton	Danson	Detective
Travis	Bailey	Carter	Detective
Dr. Rogers			Coroner
Jane	Elousie	Stradford	Lieutenant Governor
Felix			proprietor at fishing dock
Golden Goose			Name of the Yacht
Sandra		Olson	Policewoman guard
Annie	Lorie	Scots	Missing girl
Linda		Annies	older daughter
Lorie		Annies	second daughter
Harold		Zimmerman	Chicago DEA
James	Oscor	Kaizer	Sheriff of Wiggin
Abbie	Alisa	Bender	protect Alex married James
John	S.	Williams	Lawyer that was abused
Hanna		Waverly	John's mate
Angelica			Angel on the hill
Brian		Lexter	Cinci FBI Bureau Chief
Cais		Leu	Alex's Viet friend
Tracy		Hunter	Trey's Analyst

https://www.remwriter95.net/

Published by: Around the World Publishing LLC.